"Are you okay?"

"Never better." Shane grinned. "The bull barely nicked me."

She studied him critically. "You're limping."

He laughed, he couldn't help it, and lowered his voice. "I appreciate the concern, Cassidy. It means a lot to me."

"Of course I'm concerned. That was a close call."

"Is that the only reason?" He leaned in. A mere fraction at first, then more.

She drew abruptly back. "I don't know what you're implying."

"That you're worried about me because you might like me a little."

"Well, I don't."

His grin widened. "Could have fooled me."

"You always did have a big ego."

"Matched only by my..." He let the sentence drop.

"Shane!"

"Confidence," he finished with a chuckle.

"Clearly you're just fine. I don't know why I worried." Cassidy spun on her heel and stalked away.

Try as he might, Shane couldn't stop staring as she walked.

Then again, he wasn't trying very hard.

Dear Reader,

I often write about blended families. I find the skill of balancing delicate relationships makes for challenging writing and compelling reading. And adding a secret that someone doesn't want revealed ups the stakes and results in an even more interesting story. I have all those things and more in this third installment of my Reckless, Arizona series, *The Bull Rider's Son*.

While I hate to see a series end, I have to say I like this last book the best. Nothing scares a mother more than the fear of losing her child, even temporarily. Cassidy Beckett has good reason to live in dread. She never got over the heartache of her brother's abandonment when he left her to live with their father. When Shane Westcott, her son's uncle, shows up at the Easy Money Rodeo Arena, it's all Cassidy can do to prevent history from repeating itself. She must keep the identity of her son's father a secret at all costs, something that would be infinitely easier if she weren't wildly attracted to Shane.

Yes, delicate relationships. Definitely challenging and fun, and why we read romance! As always, I hope you enjoy this book. And if you're inclined to drop me a line, I always enjoy hearing from readers.

Warmest wishes,

Cathy McDavid

Facebook.com/CathyMcDavidBooks

@CathyMcDavid

CathyMcDavid.com

THE BULL RIDER'S SON

CATHY MCDAVID

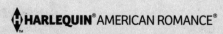

Recycling programs
for this product may
not exist in your area.

ISBN-13: 978-0-373-75575-2

The Bull Rider's Son

Copyright © 2015 by Cathy McDavid

All rights reserved. Except for use in any review, the reproduction or
utilization of this work in whole or in part in any form by any electronic,
mechanical or other means, now known or hereinafter invented, including
xerography, photocopying and recording, or in any information storage
or retrieval system, is forbidden without the written permission of the
publisher, Harlequin Enterprises Limited, 225 Duncan Mill Road,
Don Mills, Ontario M3B 3K9, Canada.

This is a work of fiction. Names, characters, places and incidents are
either the product of the author's imagination or are used fictitiously,
and any resemblance to actual persons, living or dead, business
establishments, events or locales is entirely coincidental.

This edition published by arrangement with Harlequin Books S.A.

For questions and comments about the quality of this book,
please contact us at CustomerService@Harlequin.com.

® and TM are trademarks of Harlequin Enterprises Limited or its
corporate affiliates. Trademarks indicated with ® are registered in the
United States Patent and Trademark Office, the Canadian Intellectual
Property Office and in other countries.

Printed in U.S.A.

For the past eighteen years **Cathy McDavid** has been juggling a family, a job and writing, and doing pretty well at it, except for the housecleaning part. "Mostly" retired from the corporate business world, she writes full-time from her home in Scottsdale, Arizona, near the breathtaking McDowell Mountains. Her twins have "mostly" left home, returning every now and then to raid her refrigerators. On weekends, she heads to her cabin in the mountains, always taking her laptop with her. You can visit her website at cathymcdavid.com.

Books by Cathy McDavid

Harlequin American Romance

The Accidental Sheriff
Dusty: Wild Cowboy
The Comeback Cowboy
Aidan: Loyal Cowboy

Mustang Valley

Last Chance Cowboy
Her Cowboy's Christmas Wish
Baby's First Homecoming
Cowboy for Keeps

Sweetheart, Nevada

The Rancher's Homecoming
His Christmas Sweetheart
Most Eligible Sheriff

Reckless, Arizona

More Than a Cowboy
Her Rodeo Man

Visit the Author Profile page
at Harlequin.com for more titles.

To Mike and Friday nights.

Chapter One

Few people receive a second chance in life. Shane Westcott was one of them—three times over—and he had no intention of squandering his good fortune. He was lucky to be alive, lucky to be gaining shared custody of his four-year-old daughter and lucky to have landed the job as bull manager at the Easy Money Rodeo Arena.

"Keep him moving," he called to Kenny, the young wrangler in charge of herding Wasabi from the large, open main pen into one of the smaller adjoining holding pens. It was imperative they isolate the bull from the others. "Don't let him dawdle."

The solid black Brahma-longhorn cross had other ideas and stepped slowly, almost daintily, through the gate. His actions were so far removed from his normal fiery temper, Shane hardly recognized the bull.

"He don't want to move," Kenny complained when Wasabi stopped completely.

"Tickle him on the hocks."

Kenny gawked at Shane as if he'd suggested hopping onto the bull's back and taking him for a leisurely spin. "You can't pay me enough to get in there with that monster."

The monster in question bellowed pitifully, sounding more like a calf missing his mama than an eighteen-hundred-pound bucking machine capable of launching world champions twelve feet into the air with a mere toss of his head.

"Use the rake over there," Shane instructed.

Kenny turned and, spotting the rake leaning against the back of a chute, gave a comical double take. "Well, lookie there."

Shane resisted rolling his eyes. With help like this, it was no wonder the rodeo arena needed someone competent in charge.

Grabbing hold of the rake, Kenny bent and poked the handle through an opening in the fence then tapped Wasabi on his back hocks. The bull promptly grunted with annoyance and banged his huge head into the gate hard enough to rattle the hinges.

"Again," Shane said, and the teenager complied, grimacing as he did.

Bred for bucking, twisting and spinning, Wasabi had the ability to earn money hand over fist for his new owner, but only if his injury was correctly identified, diagnosed and treated. This was Shane's chance to prove his new boss had made the right decision in hiring him.

Not a lot of pressure for his first day on the job.

"He's favoring his left front foot." Mercer Beckett, co-owner of the arena, stood beside Shane at the fence. Resting his boot on the bottom rung, he chewed a large wad of gum—a habit left over from quitting smoking years ago.

"You're wrong," Shane said. "He's favoring his shoulder."

Mercer squinted skeptically. "You don't say?"

"Watch how he hesitates after taking a step, not before."

Shane climbed the fence for a better view. He knew Wasabi personally. In fact, he'd taken his last competitive ride on the bull. If not for split-second timing and fate stepping in, Shane might have been carried away from that harrowing fall on a stretcher instead of walking away

under his own steam. He'd decided then and there to re-
tire a champion and find a new profession. Six months
had passed since, and it turned out to be the best decision
he could have made.

"Seems Doc Worthington agrees with you," Mercer
said. He'd mentioned the arena's regular veterinarian before, on their way over to the bull pen.

Shane frowned. "If he's already figured out what's
wrong with Wasabi, why'd you ask me?"

"Isn't it obvious?"

To see if Shane was worth his salt as a bull manager. Understandable. He'd been at it a mere five months. "What's
his treatment course?"

"Anti-inflammatory injections. Rest." Mercer shrugged.
"Time."

"Which you don't have."

"Our next rodeo is three weeks away. Wasabi's our
main draw. Going to be a lot of disappointed cowboys if
I have to pull him from the lineup."

Not a promising beginning for a rodeo arena with a
relatively new bucking bull program.

"Three weeks is cutting it a little close," Shane said.
"Injuries don't heal overnight."

"Joe Blackwood mentioned you worked wonders at the
Payson Rodeo Arena, and their bull had a ruptured disc."

The longtime rodeo promoter and friend of the Becketts had recommended Shane for this job. Shane didn't
want to let either man down.

"Have you heard of Guillermo Herrara?" Shane stepped
off the fence and onto the ground.

"Vaguely. He's a rodeo vet out of Dallas."

"Not just a rodeo vet. He's a specialist in bovine sports
medicine."

"There's such a thing?"

"There is. And he's had a lot of success in treating chronic joint injuries with massage therapy."

Mercer laughed. "You have got to be kidding."

Shane shrugged. "How important is it to you Wasabi is sound and ready to go in three weeks?"

"You're planning on massaging that bull's shoulder?"

"With a little help from your veterinarian."

Mercer's laugh simmered to a low chuckle. "This I have to see."

They spent another thirty minutes with Wasabi. Unlike Kenny, Shane had no qualms about crawling into the pen. True, the bull was in pain, but Shane didn't consider the threat to be too great. Mercer's only response had been to raise his brows and chew his gum faster.

"Okay," the arena owner hollered when they were done. "You can put him back now."

Kenny didn't appear any happier about returning Wasabi to the main pen than he had been about fetching him.

"Let's head to the office and start on your paperwork." Mercer led the way. "Sunny is a stickler about having all the proper payroll forms filled out."

It was well known among people in the rodeo world that Mercer and Sunny Beckett, divorced for twenty-five years, were in business together. An unusual arrangement, for sure, but a successful one. Sunny oversaw the business side of the arena and Mercer the livestock.

Their three grown children worked alongside them. Ryder, a former ad agency executive, handled the arena's marketing and promotion. Their youngest daughter, Liberty, taught riding and supervised trail rides. Cassidy, their oldest daughter and the Beckett family member Shane knew better than the others, was in charge of the bucking jackpots, team penning competitions and roping clinics.

He half hoped to see her in the office. The stab of disappointment he felt when he didn't took him by surprise. He'd always liked Cassidy. In fact, they'd dated briefly in their late teens for about a month.

In those days, both of them were focused on their rodeo careers and the relationship quickly fizzled. Some years later, she and Shane's brother Hoyt began dating. Their relationship had lasted longer and was more serious, though it, too, had ended. Shane remembered being a little jealous and thinking his brother a fool to let her go.

But that had been a long time ago. After Cassidy and Hoyt's breakup, she'd quit barrel racing altogether. Shane crossed paths with her periodically, mostly when he came to the Easy Money for a rodeo. Their chats never lasted long, he assumed because of whatever resentment she still harbored toward his brother.

"Sunny, it's a pleasure to see you again." He flashed the arena's other co-owner his best smile, which she returned along with offering him a firm handshake.

"Welcome, Shane. Come into my office. I have your employment package ready."

Mercer waited in the reception area while Shane accompanied Sunny. He thought about asking after Cassidy, then decided against it.

Once Shane was seated in the visitor's chair, Sunny handed him a slim stack of papers. "There's a lot of reading, I'm afraid. Employee policies and procedures. Withholding tax forms to complete. A noncompete agreement. Take everything home tonight and bring it back in the morning. All I need for now is the I-9 form completed and to see two forms of ID."

Shane fished his driver's license and Social Security card from his wallet.

When they were done, he asked her a few general questions about the arena. Sunny was friendlier than Shane had anticipated. He'd been warned by both Joe Blackwood and Mercer that the matriarch of the Beckett family wasn't in favor of the new bull operation. Shane had more to prove than his ability to manage. He needed to ensure the operation was run safely and profitably.

"About my daughter," he began.

"Mercer mentioned you'd be having her for visits."

"Yeah, alternating weekends."

He didn't add, *temporarily*. Eventually, Shane was hoping to have Bria for considerably longer visits. He'd need larger, more permanent living quarters than the fifth-wheel trailer that came with this job. Bria's mother had insisted, and he didn't blame her. Rodeo was no lifestyle for a four-year-old girl.

The fall from Wasabi had prompted Shane to leave the only career he'd ever known. Discovering he was a father—something Bria's mother had revealed *after* Shane quit—required him to settle down and find a new occupation. The Easy Money Rodeo Arena, the heart and soul of Reckless, Arizona, and the small town's most popular Wild West attraction, could be the place where Shane carved out his future.

"Is it against policy for me to take my daughter riding on arena horses?" he asked.

"Of course not." Sunny's expression warmed. "We have plenty of kid-friendly mounts. But you'll be required to sign a waiver. And provide proof of health insurance."

"No problem." He'd remind Judy to bring the card with her when she dropped off Bria next weekend.

Judy was usually very accommodating, and he couldn't be more grateful. It might be guilt motivating her since she had kept Bria a secret from him all those years. Or it could be she was about to get married to a guy with children of his own. Shane didn't care. All that mattered was they were working together for Bria's best interests.

"Speaking of your daughter…" Sunny rose from her chair. "I'll let Mercer show you the trailer now."

Shane shook her hand. "Thank you again for the opportunity."

"All set?" Mercer waited by the door leading to the barn, a look of expectation on his weathered and whiskered face.

Expectation, Shane noted, directed at Sunny. Not him. It was obvious Mercer cared deeply for his ex-wife. She, on the other hand, was not as easy to read.

Mercer led Shane behind the main barn to where an older-model trailer was parked in the shade. A green garden hose ran from a spigot to the hookup beside the trailer's door. A heavy-duty orange cord connected the trailer to an electrical outlet. The door stood slightly ajar and the folding metal steps were lowered.

Shane didn't need to go inside to know he'd hung his hat in far worse places than this. In fact, it was a step up from many.

Mercer handed him a key on a ring. "Make yourself at home."

"Mind if I park my truck here?" Once Shane had a look around the trailer, he'd unload his belongings and unpack.

Before Mercer could answer, his cell phone jangled. Listening in silence to the caller for several seconds, he barked, "Be right there," and disconnected. "Sorry, I have an emergency. One of the calves got tangled in some wire."

"Anything I can help with?"

"Naw." He dismissed Shane with a wave of his hand. "Get yourself settled."

Shane watched a moment as Mercer jogged in the direction of the livestock pens located on the other side of the arena. When his new boss was out of sight, Shane climbed the trailer's two steps, opened the door wide and entered his new home. His first sight was of the small but comfortable living room–dining room combo. His second sight was of the tiny kitchen.

His third sight, and the one cementing his boots to the carpeted floor, was of Cassidy Beckett, pushing aside the accordion divider separating the sleeping area from the rest of the trailer.

She swallowed a small, startled gasp, and her hand fluttered to her throat where it rested. "Sorry. I wasn't expecting you yet. Mom asked me to put fresh towels in the bathroom and change the sheets on the bed."

"You don't have to go to any trouble." The words caught in his throat before he choked them out.

Shane had always thought of Cassidy as pretty. Sometime during the intervening years she'd grown into a striking beauty with large dark eyes and shoulder-length hair the same chocolate brown shade as a wild mink.

He stopped thinking about why his brother let her go and began wondering why he shouldn't ask Cassidy out himself. No reason not to. She was exactly the kind of woman he fancied. More importantly, she had no lingering attachments to his brother—who'd married someone else shortly after he and Cassidy split. She also had a son close in age to Bria and would probably be understanding of his single-dad responsibilities.

"It's good to see you again," he said and strode forward to greet her with a hug.

Suddenly, Shane's new job had an altogether different perk. One which quite appealed to him.

THE INITIAL ALARM Cassidy experienced upon seeing Shane tripled when he swept her up in an enthusiastic embrace. It was bad enough her father had hired him. Worse that her mother insisted she stock the trailer with fresh linens. Disastrous that he'd caught her here. With him blocking the narrow passageway to the door, escape was impossible. She had no choice but to surrender to his powerful hold on her.

"Good to see you, too," she managed to reply.

He didn't immediately release her. Cassidy worried he'd sense the tension coursing through her and attempted to extract herself. He let her go long enough to take in the length of her from head to toe before hauling her against him a second time.

"You look great."

"Thanks," she mumbled, refusing to return the compliment by admitting how incredible he looked. And smelled.

Good heavens, the man had been out with the bulls for at least an hour by her estimation. He should reek to high heaven. Instead, with her face firmly planted in the crook of his shoulder, she inhaled the spicy and appealing scent of whatever aftershave he'd used this morning.

With their broad shoulders, lean, muscular builds and ruggedly chiseled profiles, both Westcott brothers were head-turning handsome. Back when the three of them were competing on the rodeo circuit, Cassidy had considered Hoyt to be the more attractive of the pair. No longer. Shane not only held his own in the looks department, he'd surpassed his older brother.

Finally, thank goodness, his grip slackened and he freed her. "How have you been, girl?"

"Umm...okay."

Girl? To her horror and chagrin, her heart gave a small flutter at the endearment he'd used during their short-lived romance. She dismissed it. Being attracted to Shane was impossible. For too many reasons to list.

"Sorry I interrupted you." She attempted to pass him. "Let me get out of your way. I'm sure you want to unpack."

"Stay a while." He didn't budge. "We can catch up."

"I promised Liberty I'd help with her riding class this afternoon." Surely her sister would forgive this one small fib, considering the circumstances.

It was then Cassidy remembered her sister didn't know the circumstances. No one did for certain except their mother, and Cassidy had sworn her to secrecy.

"That's not for another hour." Shane smiled sheepishly and—dang it all—appealingly. "Your dad mentioned the schedule earlier."

Her father. Of course, Cassidy thought with a groan. He alone was responsible for hiring Shane and throwing her life into utter turmoil.

"We have a new student signing up."

"Come on." Shane gestured to the dining table. "It's been years since we had a real talk."

It was true. Cassidy had avoided him and Hoyt like the plague, determined not to let either of them near her son, Benjie. It hadn't been easy. Shane had competed regularly until recently and often visited the Easy Money.

"Five minutes." Shane removed his cowboy hat and tossed it onto the table.

She hesitated. The one thing more dangerous than being alone with Shane was being alone with his brother. To refuse, however, might raise Shane's suspicions. She couldn't chance it.

"Okay." She slid slowly onto the bench seat, the faded upholstery on the cushions pulling at her jeans, and repeated "Five minutes" for good measure.

He plunked down across from her, a pleased grin on his face.

Cassidy swallowed. The small dining table didn't provide nearly enough distance. Shane's appeal was infinitely more potent up close. His sandy brown hair, worn longer now than when he was competing, didn't quite cover the jagged scar starting beneath his ear and disappearing inside his shirt collar—a souvenir courtesy of his last ride on Wasabi. And those green eyes, intense one second and twinkling with mirth the next, were hard to resist.

Currently, they searched her face. Cassidy tried not to show any signs of the distress weakening her knees and quickening her breath.

"What's Hoyt up to these days?" She strove to sound mildly interested, which wasn't the case.

"Same as always. Heading to a rodeo in Austin this weekend."

"Still married?"

At the spark of curiosity in Shane's eyes, she wished she'd posed the question differently. Now he'd think she cared about Hoyt's marital state. Well, she did. But not for *that* reason.

"He and Cheryl are doing fine. Bought a house in Jackson Hole last year."

Jackson Hole. In Wyoming. Good, Cassidy thought. Plenty far from Reckless, Arizona.

"Any kids yet?" She cursed herself for needing to know.

"Nope." Shane shrugged. "Still trying. Hoyt wants a big family. Or so he says."

A jolt shot through her. She attempted to hide it with a show of nonchalance. "Tell me about your daughter."

Shane instantly brightened. "Bria's four. Not sure yet if she wants to be a princess or a soccer player when she grows up."

"What? No cowgirl?"

"I'm hoping to change her mind."

Cassidy's son, Benjie, wanted to be a champion bull rider. Like his grandfather before him and, unbeknownst to all but Cassidy and her mother, like his father and Uncle Shane.

She quickly shoved her hands beneath the table before Shane spotted them shaking. How was she ever going to keep him from finding out about Benjie and telling Hoyt? She vowed to find a way.

There were those who'd disagree, claiming she should have told Hoyt from the beginning about Benjie. That he had a right to know. Others, admittedly not many, who would side with her. It wasn't just Hoyt's nomadic lifestyle and partying ways, which had been one of the reasons for their breakup. Cassidy couldn't take the chance of him fighting for, and probably winning, joint custody of Benjie.

She'd seen firsthand how parents living in separate towns divided a family. When her brother, Ryder, had turned fourteen, he'd left to live with their father. Up until last fall, Ryder had rarely seen or spoken to Cassidy, Liberty and their mother. Their father's return had reunited the Becketts, but they were far from being a family. Not in the truest sense. Too much hurt and betrayal, and too many lies littered their past.

No way, no how, was she putting her son through the same broken childhood she'd endured. She would not suffer the same heartbreak that had devastated her mother when they'd lost Ryder. And it would happen. Of that, Cassidy was certain.

"Mom mentioned Bria will be visiting soon." Cassidy forced a smile.

Shane, on the other hand, beamed. "Every other weekend to start."

To start? Was he planning on obtaining full custody of his daughter? Cassidy's anxiety increased. If Hoyt followed his brother's example...

She pushed the unpleasant thought away. "She's close by, then?"

"Mesa."

"Ah." A forty-five-minute drive.

"That's why I accepted this job." A glint lit his eyes

as his gaze focused on her. "Now I have even more incentive."

Oh, dear. Cassidy steeled herself, determined to resist him. "Bria's mom is okay with you taking her more often?"

"Judy's been great. She wants Bria and me to have a relationship."

"But she lied to you about having a child."

The uncanny similarities between Benjie and Bria weren't lost on Cassidy.

"I understand her reasons," Shane said. "I wasn't what you'd call good father material. Now that I've quit my wild ways and found a job which keeps me in one place, Judy's willing to work with me."

His brother, too, had quit his wild ways to become a rodeo announcer, but Cassidy didn't feel inclined to work with him. Not yet, and maybe not ever.

"It can't be easy for you, seeing Wasabi every day."

"He's just another bull under my care."

Her gaze was automatically drawn to his scar. She'd seen the pictures posted on their mutual friends' Facebook pages. The gash, requiring forty-four stitches, traveled from beneath his right ear, down his neck to his chest. Miraculously, Wasabi's hoof had just missed an artery. Otherwise, Shane might have bled out.

"I'm glad you're all right." Her voice unwittingly softened.

Shane responded with a heart-melting smile. No surprise he'd inspired a legion of female fans during his years on the circuit. Was that the reason for Bria's mother's secrecy? It wouldn't surprise Cassidy.

"Not my day to die," Shane said matter-of-factly.

"All the same, it was a terrible fall. How can you bear to look at Wasabi?" Cassidy still shuddered when she passed the well house, even though the accident involving her and her father happened twenty-five years ago.

Like Shane, she'd walked away when things might have gone horribly different.

He shrugged. "He was just doing his job. Like any bull. I didn't take it personally."

More charm. He could certainly lay it on thick. And Cassidy was far more susceptible than she liked.

She abruptly stood. "I need to go."

Reaching for his cowboy hat, he also stood and waited for her to leave first. "Drop by anytime." The invitation was innocent. Not so his tone, which hinted at something else altogether.

When she spoke, *her* tone was all business. "If you need something, let me know."

"How about having dinner with me?"

She blinked. He didn't just ask her on a date, did he? "I beg your pardon?"

"Your dad mentioned a couple good restaurants in town. I could use someone to show me around. Help me get the lay of the land. Seeing as we'll be working together—"

She shook her head. "Benjie, my son, has homework tonight."

"You could bring him along."

"Thanks, but no. He has enough trouble with school as it is. I'd never get him to finish his homework if we went to dinner first."

"Maybe another night this week."

Did the man never give up? "We'll see," she said, planning to stall him indefinitely.

Outside the trailer she allowed herself two full seconds to gather her wits before heading to the arena in search of her sister. Should Shane come searching for her, he'd find Cassidy doing exactly what she said, helping with the riding lesson.

Fortunately, Liberty was there, talking to a student's

mother. She finished just as Cassidy approached and met her halfway.

"What's wrong?" Liberty asked.

Cassidy shook her head. "Nothing."

"You look like you've seen a ghost."

Not a ghost. The brother of one, perhaps. "I was talking to our new bull manager."

"Shane? Do tell."

Cassidy planted her hands on her hips. "What does that mean?"

"He's a nice-looking guy."

"We work at a rodeo arena. There are a lot of nice-looking guys here."

"But none of them have ever left you flustered. Didn't you two date once?"

Cassidy ignored the question. "I'm not flustered. I'm annoyed. I have a lot to do and can't afford the time it takes to babysit a new employee."

"Right." Liberty laughed gaily before turning on her heel and leaving Cassidy to stew alone.

She hated it when her baby sister was right.

Chapter Two

Seven-point-three seconds into his ride, the young cowboy came flying off the bull's back. He dropped to his knees as the buzzer sounded, then pitched forward onto his face. Recovering, he pushed to his feet, grabbed his fallen hat and dusted off his jeans, a fierce scowl on his face.

Cassidy couldn't be sure if he was mad at himself for failing to reach the full eight seconds required to qualify or if he was in pain. Perhaps a little of both. He hobbled slightly on his walk of shame from the arena. Behind him, a trio of wranglers chased the bull to the far end and through a gate. A fourth wrangler swung the gate shut on the great beast's heels.

Score: bull one, cowboy zero.

"Better luck next time," a buddy hailed from the fence where he'd been watching.

A second pal slapped the cowboy on the back while a third offered him a bottled water and hearty condolences.

Moving as a group, the two dozen participants from the Tuesday night jackpot slowly made their way to the open area where either their families, friends or pickup trucks waited.

Cassidy switched off her handheld radio and tucked her clipboard beneath her arm. She, too, was almost done for the evening.

Bull-riding jackpots, along with bucking horse, calf roping and steer-wrestling competitions, were popular events at the Easy Money. Especially in the weeks preceding a rodeo. If a participant performed well, he could earn enough winnings to cover his entry fees and perhaps a little extra. If not, well, at least he got in some good practice.

Tonight, Shane had worked closely with Cassidy's father, learning the ins and outs. He also studied each bull, noting the personalities and traits of those new to him and re-familiarizing himself with those he'd previously ridden.

Cassidy knew this for a fact because she'd taken her eyes off him only long enough to perform her tasks of calling out the participants' names and communicating with her sister in the announcer's booth. Even now she had to look away for fear of Shane catching her staring at him with doe eyes. Again. He had already, twice.

Damn, damn, damn. Why did her father have to hire Shane Westcott of all people? She should have said something when she'd had the chance. But, then, she would have had to tell her father why, and that was out of the question.

Okay, Shane was competent at his new job. Cassidy noticed he took time to converse with each cowboy, offering tips and pointers and, more importantly, listening to the cowboy talk about his ride.

Shane entered every piece of information into a small spiral notebook he constantly removed and replaced in his shirt's front pocket. No fancy-schmancy handheld electronic device for him.

Somehow, Cassidy thought that fitting. Shane didn't strike her as a high-tech kind of guy. No wonder he and her father got along like twins separated at birth.

They also dressed alike, though Shane's shirt fit his

broad shoulders better and his jeans hugged his narrow hips with drool-worthy closeness.

Stop looking at him!

Slamming her mouth shut, Cassidy wheeled around, intending to return the handheld radio to the registration booth and do a final total on tonight's runs. Instead, she came face-to-face with her mother.

"Keep staring at him like that and you're going to draw attention to yourself."

"I'm not staring," Cassidy insisted.

"Sure. And I'm a natural blonde."

"You *are* a natural blonde."

"Was. These days, my color is courtesy of Pizzazz Hair Salon." Her mother linked an arm through Cassidy's and led her away from the chutes. "Come on. Let's get out of here before he's any the wiser."

"It's not what you think."

"You did date once."

"I'm just curious."

"About him or Hoyt?"

"Not so loud," Cassidy admonished and glanced nervously about. No one appeared to have heard, but she couldn't be too careful. "Hoyt, of course," she continued in a half whisper. "I asked Shane about him the other day."

"And?"

"He's still married. Still childless. The good thing is, he and his wife bought a house in Jackson Hole."

The two of them walked to the registration booth. There Cassidy removed the wristband key ring she wore and unlocked the door. Breathing a sigh of relief, she entered the one-room modified office. Finally, they were out of earshot.

"Just because he has no children," her mother said, "doesn't automatically mean he'd seek custody of Benjie."

"You can't be serious." Cassidy entered numbers on a

ten-key calculator, tallying the evening's scores for her father. And probably, Shane as well. She'd have to explain their system to him.

Drat. Yet another reason for them to work together. She paused and leaned against the counter. "To quote Shane, 'Hoyt wants a big family.'"

"Me not telling your dad about Liberty is no reason for you to keep Hoyt in the dark regarding Benjie."

Cassidy gawked at her mother. "I thought you were on my side."

"I am on your side and will support any decision you make."

"Except now that Dad's back, and he and Liberty are all cozy and comfy, you're having second thoughts."

"I've always had regrets. It wasn't an easy decision to make, lying all these years."

The story was well known throughout Reckless and by plenty of others in the rodeo world. Sunny Beckett sent her husband and business partner packing when his acute alcoholism nearly ruined them, personally and financially. What she didn't tell him, or anyone else, was that she had been pregnant with their third child. Rather, she lied about the father's identity, claiming he was some cowboy passing through.

Then, last summer, Liberty had accidentally discovered Mercer Beckett was her biological father and tracked him down. He used a reconciliation with her to worm his way back into the lives of his ex-wife and daughters.

One good thing *had* happened in the wake of Mercer's return. Cassidy's brother, Ryder, also came home. They still didn't agree on their father—Ryder trusted their father's sobriety and she didn't—but otherwise the two of them had grown close during the last few months.

How could they not? Ryder was engaged to Cassidy's best friend, Tatum Mayweather, after all. Cassidy hadn't seen that one coming, but she was pleased for both her brother and best friend. They proved differences were superficial when it came to love.

Theirs was actually the second of two upcoming Beckett weddings. Liberty was also engaged. To Deacon McCrea, a former employee of the arena and now their legal counsel. Cassidy, conversely, remained single and planned to stay that way.

She'd been asked to be maid of honor at both affairs, the dates of which had recently been set for this summer and fall respectively. She would be pretty busy during the coming months, assisting with the thousand and one details, hosting bridal showers and making short day trips to pick out dresses.

Thank goodness she didn't need to worry about her parents. Since his return, her father had made it clear he was still in love with her mother and intended to remarry her. So far, her mother was resisting. One of her parents, at least, was behaving sensibly.

"Well, I have no regrets." Cassidy powered off the ten-key calculator and tore loose the paper tape.

"Hoyt has a right to know he's a father," her mother said.

"And Dad didn't?"

"You deserve child support."

"I don't see the big deal. You didn't get any from Dad for Liberty and managed just fine."

Her mother compressed her lips in a show of impatience. "That's not entirely true and you know it. He didn't take any money for his share of the arena all those years—which is basically the same as paying child support."

"He stole Ryder from us."

"Ryder went to live with him when he was old enough to legally choose."

Cassidy's chest grew tight making it hard to breathe. "I won't lose Benjie."

And there it was. The crux of the matter. Cassidy's greatest fear. What would happen if she told Hoyt about Benjie? Even if he didn't come after her for some sort of custody, Benjie could one day decide he'd rather live with his father and leave her just like Ryder.

"Shane's not stupid." Her mother's manner was less judgmental and more sympathetic. "He's bound to put two and two together."

"Not if I can help it."

"You can't keep Benjie hidden from him forever. They'll meet eventually. What if Shane tells Hoyt?"

"I'll lie if I have to." Leave Reckless if necessary.

"You've been lucky so far. One day Benjie's going to ask about his father, and you won't be able to put him off like you have in the past."

"I'll figure something out."

"Cassidy—"

"Believe me, Mom, I've weighed the pros and cons. I'm not ready to tell Benjie or Hoyt."

Her mother sighed. "You didn't always feel that way."

No, she hadn't. When she was eight months pregnant Cassidy had gone so far as to locate Hoyt and drive to where he was living, only to learn he was engaged to Cheryl, a young widow who'd lost her first husband unexpectedly. Putting herself in Cheryl's shoes, Cassidy had turned around and driven back to Reckless. She wouldn't be a home wrecker. Been there, done that, and she refused to compound the guilt she already bore.

"I came to my senses."

As if reading Cassidy's thoughts, her mother said, "You weren't the reason I divorced your father."

"I know."

"Do you? Really?"

"He was a drunk. If you hadn't divorced him, he'd have driven the arena into bankruptcy. I may have been ten, but I remember. Everything."

The smell of alcohol clinging to him like a layer of heavy sweat. Finding him passed out in the back of his pickup truck behind the barn. Or on the living room couch if he managed to stagger inside. Once in the middle of the kitchen floor. Twice in the chaise lounge on the back patio when her mother had banished him from the house.

Worst of all were the outbursts, which, to this day, still rang in her ears. The yelling. The fights. The breaking down into gut-wrenching sobs, his and her mother's. The constant apologies.

"He regrets the accident."

Cassidy wheeled on her mother. "He could have killed me. And himself."

"I'm not defending him."

"Sounds like you are." She wiped at the tears springing to her eyes, angry at herself for letting her emotions get the best of her.

"What's important is that you weren't hurt. Either of you. Just scared. No less than I was, trust me."

Memories surfaced. They were never far away. Especially since her father's return.

One night, shortly before her parents' marriage imploded, her father fetched her from a friend's house when her mother couldn't get away. The people lived less than a mile away. Nonetheless, he shouldn't have been driving. Cassidy refused to go with him at first. When he raised his voice, she acquiesced rather than have him cause a scene in front of her friend.

Misjudging the distance, he ran the truck into the well house. Granted, they weren't going fast, twenty-five miles an hour at most, and the well house suffered the most damage. There was a small dent on the truck's front fender. Cassidy's seat belt saved her from injury.

When the truck rolled to a stop, she jumped out the door and sprinted the entire way to the house, yelling at her mother to make her father leave. Two weeks later, her mother did.

At first Cassidy had been glad. Good riddance. Then, seeing how miserable her mother and brother were, she was consumed by guilt. The feeling intensified when, two years later, Ryder left. When she was older, she'd wondered if her reaction to the accident had driven her mother into the arms of another man within days after her father left. Learning that was all a lie had affected Cassidy more than she let on.

"I put up with the drinking and the bad business decisions," her mother continued. "But I couldn't let him endanger my children. Once the trust is gone, there's no getting it back."

"You trust him now. At least, you act like you do. You let him purchase the bulls when you swore we'd never own them again." And that purchase had led her father to hiring Shane.

"There's no letting or not letting," her mother said. "We're partners. An arrangement requiring give and take on both sides."

"What did he give?" From where Cassidy stood, her mother had done all the compromising.

"He agreed to put money aside for Benjie's college education."

Cassidy was taken aback, especially when her mother named the amount.

"His own personal money," her mother added. "Not the arena's."

She quickly recovered. "He can't buy my affections.

Or my forgiveness. And he can't buy off his responsibility for what happened."

"Did it ever occur to you that he's simply doing something nice for his grandson? He does love the boy. And Benjie adores him."

He did, which rankled Cassidy to no end. "I'll tell him no."

"You can't stop him. It's his money. He can do with it what he wants. And when the time comes, Benjie can accept it, with or without your consent."

Cassidy liked that less.

During these past six months her life had been slowly spiraling out of control. First her father returned. Then both her siblings met their future spouses. Lastly her father had hired Shane.

Cassidy vowed anew to keep her son from his uncle's path as much as possible. The benefit would be twofold. In addition to keeping the identity of Benjie's father a secret, she'd quell this wild and inexplicable attraction to Shane. Anything else was unacceptable.

"ATTA BOY," SHANE CROONED. "Steady now."

Wasabi swayed from side to side, but managed to remain standing—which was a good thing. If the bull collasped onto all fours, his massive weight could compress his lungs and cut off his breathing. It was imperative that every move be precisely executed, every step accomplished at the exact right moment or Wasabi might die.

"We're done," Doc Worthington said, visibly relaxing as the tranquilizer took effect.

Getting the bull sedated had been a tricky process, to say the least. With few choices, and to be as humane as possible, the Becketts' vet had used a tranquilizer gun, aiming the feather-tipped dart at Wasabi's muscular hindquarters. The bull hadn't felt a thing.

Turned out, the initial dose hadn't been strong enough, and the vet had to administer a second one, which had worried Shane. Stress and excitement could cause the tranquilizer to run through the bull's system at an incredible rate. Shane had once seen a bull require five doses.

Now, he carefully monitored the entire procedure from his place beside the wizened country vet. So far, so good, and his respect for the older man grew.

Two of the arena's most capable wranglers had been recruited to act as spotters, along with Mercer. If Shane appeared to be in any trouble during the bull's massage therapy, they'd jump right in. Shane was glad for their presence. Despite his show of confidence, this type of therapy was relatively new to him. A phone call yesterday with the bovine sports medicine specialist had yielded some helpful advice.

The older veterinarian considered Shane a bit crazy to take this on, especially since he had limited experience.

Yes, there were risks. In more ways than one. Shane might get injured, or, worse, he could make a fool of himself in the eyes of his new employer and possibly lose his job.

"You ready?" Mercer called from the sidelines.

"Let's do it." Taking a fortifying breath, Shane crawled through the fence rails.

"There's still time to tie him up."

"I don't want to upset him more than he already is."

Shane didn't have long. Twenty minutes at most before Wasabi came out of the sedation. No telling how the bull would react. Dazed and disoriented, he'd likely attack the nearest object with horns or hooves. In this case, Shane.

Straightening, he surveyed his surroundings before slowly approaching Wasabi. A small crowd had gathered to watch from a safe distance, Cassidy among them. Their gazes briefly connected before Shane looked away. He couldn't afford any distractions, and Cassidy was a big one.

Since their encounter in the trailer four days ago, it seemed as though she'd made it her mission to avoid him. Often, like at last night's bull riding jackpot, he'd sensed her presence, only to turn and find her staring at him or, more often, quickly averting her head.

She was obviously drawn to him, if nothing else, out of curiosity. And the feeling was mutual.

Why, then, did she run for the hills every time he approached? Her behavior just piqued his interest further, and Shane wasn't a man to be put off indefinitely.

"Watch it," Mercer hollered when Wasabi opened his bleary eyes and swung his head clumsily to the side. Mercer, along with the two wranglers, had formed a circle around Wasabi and Shane. "Maybe you should dose him again," he said to the vet.

"I don't dare. Not unless you have a crane handy we can use to lift him."

That elicited a round of nervous chuckles from the wranglers. They, too, were on high alert.

A moment later, the bull calmed, and his eyes drifted closed. He rumbled as if snoring. Shane waited another minute, positioning himself near Wasabi's shoulder, avoiding both the bull's hind end and head, either of which could be deadly.

When the bull didn't react, he tentatively stroked Wasabi's back. Other than a slight twitch, the animal remained motionless. Growing bolder, Shane removed first one, then the second dart. Wasabi continued sleeping, and Shane skimmed his palm down the bull's thick neck to his shoulder. Probing gently, he searched for any lumps, swelling or other signs of a contusion. Wasabi's injury could have been the result of a kick from another bull, requiring a potentially different course of treatment.

"Find anything?" Doc Worthington asked.

"Nothing yet." Shane increased the pressure, kneading methodically.

Wasabi snorted lustily. A moment later, he quieted.

"He probably just sustained a sprain."

In Shane's opinion, the vet was being optimistic. Wasabi could have a torn tendon or ligament. Trauma of that nature would end his career.

"Guess we'll know soon enough," Mercer said.

They would, if Wasabi didn't improve quickly. Like, within days.

Knowing he had little time left, Shane continued with the massage. It might be his imagination, or wishful thinking, but he swore the bull relaxed beneath his touch.

"Get the tape," he said.

Mercer delivered the roll from the vet. During Shane's phone call yesterday, the bovine sports medicine specialist had recommended elastic therapeutic tape, the same type human athletes used for their injuries. Wasabi would look a little funny, but if it helped, who cared?

Just as Shane finished affixing the last strip, the bull started to rouse.

Doc Worthington raised his tranquilizer gun. "I can dose him again."

"Don't bother, I'm done."

More correctly, Wasabi was done. Grunting angrily, he jabbed the empty air in front of him with his horns. Shane jumped out of the way, though the dazed bull missed him by a mile.

The reprieve didn't last. Wasabi awakened quickly and, finding himself confronted by hated humans, charged the closest one, which happened to be Shane. And, like that, the race was on.

Shane bolted for the fence. From the corner of his eye, he saw Mercer and the wranglers attempting to distract

Wasabi. The bull ignored all but his tormenter and bore down on Shane, his loping gait growing steadier and faster by the second.

"Look at him move." Doc Worthington slapped his thigh. "He feels better already."

At the moment, it was little consolation to Shane that his efforts had yielded the desired results.

With the fence in sight, he executed a high-flying leap. Grabbing the top railing, he hurled himself up and over and onto the other side, landing with a loud thud. Only then did he notice the sharp pain shooting up his left calf.

Wasabi had clipped him in the leg. Nothing was torn, either his jeans or his flesh, but Shane would be sore for the next few days.

Mercer ambled over to check on Shane. "I say we call it a tie."

Doc Worthington chuckled. "Or a payback."

Shane called himself plain lucky. "Anyone see what happened to the roll of therapeutic tape?" His last recollection was of it sailing out of his hand.

"In the dirt." Mercer hitched his chin at the holding pen. "We'll get it later when the coast is clear."

The two wranglers had convinced Wasabi that his interests were best served back in the main pen with the other bulls and not causing trouble for them.

"My hat's off to you, young man." Doc Worthington eyed Shane's leg. "You all right?"

"Fine." He glanced at the crowd, which had shrunk to a small gathering. Good, Shane thought. His leg did hurt, and the fewer people who knew it, the better.

All at once, Cassidy rounded the chutes, passing her father and the vet on their way to the pen, and made straight for him. It was a nice change from her recent habit of avoidance. The expression of concern on her pretty face made him almost forget about the pain shooting up his leg.

"Are you okay?" she asked in a rush.

"Never better."

"I'm serious, Shane."

"He barely nicked me."

She studied him critically, her eyes traveling from his head to his boots. "You're limping."

He grinned, he couldn't help it, and lowered his voice. "I appreciate the concern, Cassidy. It means a lot to me."

"Of course I'm concerned. You had a close call."

"Any other reason?" He leaned in. A mere fraction at first, then more.

She abruptly drew back. "I don't know what you're implying."

"I'm thinking you're worried about me because you might like me a little."

"Well, I don't."

His grin widened. "Could have fooled me."

"I mean, I do like you. As a fellow employee." Her cheeks flushed, and she tripped over her words. "And as an old friend."

He'd flustered her, and though it shouldn't, the thought pleased him. "Right."

"You always had a big ego."

"Matched only by my…." He let the sentence drop.

"Shane!"

"Confidence," he finished with a chuckle.

"I guess you are okay. Don't know why I worried."

She spun and would have left him in the dust if he hadn't grabbed her arm and pulled her swiftly to him.

"Thanks." Lowering his head, he pressed his lips to her cheek, letting them linger.

The contact wasn't much. Not as far as kisses went. No more than a light caress. Yet, it sent a shock wave coursing through him with the kick of a lightning bolt.

She must have felt a similar shock, for she let out a soft

"Oh" and, for one incredible moment, melted against him. The next instant, she tensed. "I—I have to g-go."

"Why, Cassidy?" He searched her face. To his surprise and concern, he noted fear in her eyes. "What are you afraid of?"

"Nothing."

He wanted to contradict her, but this wasn't the time or place. Not with her acting like a skittish colt and not with her father standing close by, watching the two of them like, well, like a father watches a man who's just kissed his daughter on the cheek.

What would Mercer think if he knew of Shane's attraction to Cassidy? He might approve. Then again, he might oppose it.

Maybe Shane should take a moment and step back from the situation. This job was too important for him to mess up right out of the gate.

The thrill of his encounter with Cassidy faded. Unfortunately, his attraction to her didn't. Try as he might, Shane couldn't stop staring as she walked away.

Then again, he wasn't trying very hard.

Chapter Three

"I sure appreciate the use of ole Skittles." Shane tugged on the brim of Benjie's too-big cowboy hat. "I know it's rough sometimes, letting someone else ride your horse." He lifted his daughter and planted her on Skittles's broad back, then faced Benjie again. "Bria will treat him right, I promise."

"It's okay." The boy kicked at the ground with the toe of his boot, leaving behind a large gouge in the dirt. "I can ride Rusty."

Cassidy bit her lower lip to keep herself from speaking. She knew how much her son disliked riding the potbellied, swaybacked mule. Not because Rusty was mean or difficult or stubborn, as were many of his breed. But because he wasn't a horse. That, in Benjie's opinion, made him the object of ridicule from his peers. Like a kid forced to wear no-name sneakers while everyone else in school owned expensive, celebrity-endorsed athletic shoes.

Cassidy had been getting plenty of flak from Benjie this past school semester. He complained nonstop about his discount store footwear. The thing was, she didn't have money to spare for nonessentials.

Her mother's words came back to haunt her. If she told Hoyt about Benjie, she'd be able to collect child support from him. Possibly for the years since Benjie's birth.

No, no, no. She wasn't about to share, much less risk losing, custody of her son. And Hoyt would no doubt insist on some form of custody.

"You need a leg up, too?" Shane asked Benjie.

"I got it." Nimble as a monkey, Benjie grabbed the side of the saddle and scrambled up onto Rusty's back.

"Good job."

Though Benjie would argue differently, Skittles was barely better than the mule. One of the arena's oldest mounts, the horse's slow, steady gait and docile personality made him perfect for a novice like Bria. Truthfully, Benjie was ready for a more advanced horse. But he loved Skittles and was loath to part with his pal.

"I want to go, Daddy," Bria exclaimed gleefully and jiggled her turquoise cowboy boots.

A tad on the chubby side, she sported a generous mop of curly brown hair and an impish grin that reminded Cassidy a lot of Shane.

"Okay, okay. Give me a second." Shane patted Benjie's leg. "You want to ride in the arena or come with us to the round pen?"

"With you." Benjie gazed longingly at Skittles, not at Bria, who was combing her fingers through the old horse's stringy mane.

"If it's okay with your mother." Shane glanced at Cassidy, his green eyes twinkling.

She knew at once he'd been aware of her scrutiny the entire time and said nothing. Guess she wasn't nearly as clever as she thought.

Rather than avoiding him, as was her plan when he'd first arrived, she'd gone about the arena with a business-as-usual approach these past few days. She refused to let him think their kiss had been anything other than mild and meaningless.

Truth be told, it had rocked her to her core. She couldn't

remember a time when a simple peck on the cheek had turned her limbs to liquid.

Maybe her mother was right when she said Cassidy had gone too long without dating. What other reason could there be for her racing heart every time he neared?

Cassidy's view of Shane, Bria and Benjie was obstructed when a woman astride a leggy thoroughbred rode up beside her.

"Cassidy, dearie, can you help me adjust my stirrups? They're a little long."

"Sure," she answered automatically and did as requested.

"Mom," Benjie hollered as if she'd been swallowed whole and not momentarily out of sight. "Can I go with Mr. Shane?"

The name was a compromise. Cassidy insisted her son address adults formally, one of the few holdovers from her father's strict teachings. Shane, however, wanted Benjie to call him by his first name.

She stepped around the horse and into view. What if Shane asked Benjie about his father? Better she was there to intercede. Then again, what if her going sent Shane the wrong message about them? Cassidy couldn't decide on the lesser evil.

"You're welcome to join us," Shane said affably. "If you're worried about him."

"I'm not worried." Not about Benjie.

"Then come on. The more the merrier."

"Um, I need to, ah…"

The woman on the thoroughbred leaned over her horse's neck. "For Pete's sake, go with him," she said in a loud whisper. "Don't ever turn down an invitation from a handsome man."

Seventy, if she was a day, the woman was a regular at the Easy Money and one of their few English hunter-jumper riders. Rumor had it she'd been married—and divorced—four times.

"Mom," Benjie pleaded.

Feeling pressured from all sides, Cassidy relented. "Okay, fine."

"Good decision," the woman said. "You won't regret it." Pulling on the reins, she turned her horse away and nudged him into a trot.

Wrong, Cassidy thought as she caught up with Shane and saw his satisfied grin. She regretted it already.

He walked beside his daughter, holding on to the side of Skittles's bridle. He didn't look over at Cassidy, which somehow irritated her all the more. What? Invite her and then ignore her? The next instant she reminded herself she couldn't care less. She had no interest in him.

Luckily, or unluckily, depending on one's opinion, no one was using the round pen. Benjie, familiar with the drill, entered the pen first and rode Rusty in a clockwise circle.

Cassidy tugged her short denim jacket snugger around her waist, the gesture the result of nerves and not the cool January breeze blowing in from the west.

"Daddy, I want to ride by myself," Bria said, her eyes on Benjie. "I can do it."

"In a minute. First, we need to get Skittles used to the pen."

The old horse couldn't be more used to the bull pen if he'd been born in it. Shane, Cassidy realized, was being protective, but not so protective he smothered Bria. He also engaged Benjie in friendly conversation. Her son responded as he always did to attention from cowboys at the arena. He lit up.

Did Benjie miss having a father in his life? Was she wrong to deny him?

"Race you." He passed Bria at a slow, bumpy trot.

"No, Benjie," Cassidy warned. She'd climbed the fence to a built-in bench seat, installed so parents and instructors could sit comfortably while monitoring the goings-on in the pen. "Bria isn't ready to race yet."

"But I want to," the little girl protested and kicked Skittles in the sides. The saddle's wide, thick cinch prevented her boots from making any real contact.

Like father, like daughter, Cassidy decided. The little girl was fearless. Shane had always been like that. The quality had earned him a world championship bull-riding title on three separate occasions. It had also darn near cost him his life.

Shane brought Skittles to a stop. "If you promise not to race," he told Bria, "you can fly solo."

The little girl stopped giggling in order to stare at him, an expression of bewilderment on her cherub face. "I'm not flying, Daddy. I'm riding."

"Yes, you are. And doing well, I might add."

He adjusted the reins, placing them firmly between her plump fingers. "Don't let go and don't move your hands all over the place. You'll pull on Skittles's mouth, and he won't like it."

Shane continued instructing his daughter for several minutes until she was fidgeting with excitement.

"Daddy," she whined. "I'm ready."

"All right." He stepped back and let her go.

Cassidy could see the struggle on his face. As a parent, she understood what he was going through. It wasn't easy, giving up control. Even, evidently, for Shane, who'd been a father only these last four months.

Bria completed her first circuit on her own with no mishaps. A second and third progressed just as smoothly, considering Benjie followed closely, daring her to go faster. Cassidy hadn't been aware that she'd let her thoughts drift until the bench shifted beneath her. With a loud creak, Shane plopped down.

Right beside her. She hadn't realized how small the seat was. Her pulse quickly soared. Really?

Cassidy pretended Shane's proximity made no difference to her. "She's a chip off the old block."

Indeed, Bria took to horse riding as one might expect from the offspring of a rodeo champion.

"Not bad for a first time out."

"Her mother doesn't ride?" It seemed a reasonable question to Cassidy and not her being nosy, though she was.

"Never been on a horse."

"Huh. I take it you didn't meet her on the circuit."

He leaned back, pushing his cowboy hat off his face and giving her a less obstructed view of his profile. His strong, rugged features were pronounced in the bright afternoon sun, as was his scar. Both stole her breath.

"Actually, I did. Right here. She and a friend came to the Wild West Days Rodeo."

"Wow." Cassidy hadn't noticed his interest in anyone. Then again, she'd steered clear of Shane during the rodeos he'd attended. Less chance of people talking about her son and him hearing. "Were you angry with Judy for not telling you about Bria?"

Of all the disagreements Cassidy's parents had had since her father's return, not one had been about her mother lying to him about being Liberty's father. Why was that? Surely, he was angry. She could easily imagine how furious Hoyt would be with her if he discovered her deception.

"Yeah," Shane admitted, "at first, I was angry." His tone gentled. "I got over it once I met Bria."

Cassidy doubted Hoyt would be as forgiving. Her glance returned to Bria. "She's adorable."

"She's something else, all right. I was scared to death she'd hate me. Be mad at me for abandoning her all these years."

"How could she? You didn't know about her."

"I wasn't sure she'd understand. But turns out I didn't need to worry. We hit it off from the start. Like she'd always been a part of my life."

"Was she upset with her mother?" That possibility concerned Cassidy almost as much.

"No. Judy and I concocted a story to tell her. She accepted it. I suppose because she's four."

Like Cassidy's sister. Liberty had accepted the story their mother had made up. Also like Benjie, when Cassidy put off his occasional queries.

"And Judy's willing to share custody with you?"

Shane gave Cassidy a curious look. "She is."

When he didn't ask why Cassidy wanted to know, she pushed on. "What changed her mind?"

He raised his eyebrows, his curiosity noticeably increased. Still, he didn't ask. "The accident and me walking away from rodeoing. When I decided to settle down, she thought maybe I'd grown up enough to be a father."

"Have you?"

He laughed good-naturedly. "Depends on who you ask."

"I think you have," Cassidy said, quite seriously. "You're not the same man I once knew."

"Thank you. I'll take that as a compliment."

"I meant it as one."

A spark of attraction flashed in his eyes, causing her breath to hitch. They were close. So close she could discern each and every laugh line bracketing his eyes. Feel the raw energy emanating from him. Sense the weighty pull of their mutual attraction. It wasn't easy to resist.

"What about Benjie's father?" he asked. "Is he in the picture?"

"He isn't."

And, like that, the attraction fizzled. Shane had ventured into forbidden territory.

"Sorry," she said, "I have to go. *We* have to go. Benjie," she called to her son. "Grandma's fixing dinner."

"Aw, Mom. Not yet."

Cassidy stood—and realized too late she was caught between Shane's knees and the fence railing. She couldn't pass unless he allowed it. Would he? Her gaze was drawn to his handsome face.

"Stay," he said in a voice like warm honey. "Please."

"We can't."

"You haven't given me a chance to apologize."

Before she could ask what for, two high-pitched squeals split the air. The first from Skittles, the second from Bria. In a flash, Shane vaulted from the bench. Cassidy grabbed the wooden seat before losing her balance. She twisted sideways just in time to see him reach Skittles and his daughter's side.

"I'm sorry." Benjie hung his head.

"It's all right, buddy." Shane held Bria tight in his arms. "No harm done."

Indeed, his daughter had quickly calmed down once she realized Skittles had merely taken a brisk hop-step when Benjie tugged on his tail.

"It's not okay." Cassidy came up beside him, her mouth tight. "He was teasing her horse. That's against arena rules and *my* rules."

"She's fine," Shane insisted. "And, besides, he apologized."

"Just because she's not hurt is no excuse for what he did."

Something was off in Cassidy's tone. Shane couldn't

quite put his finger on it. As if she was talking about something other than her son and the teasing incident.

"All right. Then how 'bout we punish him? One hour of mucking bull manure after school tomorrow."

Cassidy nodded in agreement. "Seems fitting."

"Do I have to?" Benjie pouted.

"Yes, you do, young man."

Bria giggled. "Ha, ha. You have to clean up cow poo."

Shane set her back atop Skittles. When he patted the horse's rump, the pair moseyed off.

Benjie followed on Rusty, his attitude adjusted.

"He's just being a boy," Shane told Cassidy.

"A misbehaving boy."

Rather than returning to the bench, he and Cassidy exited through the gate and continued watching from outside the round pen. He was glad to see she'd forgotten about leaving. For the moment, at least. Experience had taught him she'd flee at the tiniest provocation.

Shane struggled to repress a smile. The women he typically met on the circuit were transparent, making their wants and wishes crystal clear. Cassidy, on the other hand, was a mystery. He liked that about her. Then again, he'd always appreciated a challenge.

Since she hadn't brought up his apology, he did. "I'm sorry about the kiss the other day. I got carried away."

"I've forgotten all about it."

"Why don't I believe you?"

"No big deal, Shane."

Wasn't it? He'd felt something when his lips brushed her cheek. A rather enjoyable, no, exciting, sensation unlike any before. He'd been certain she'd felt it, too.

"In any case, I was out of line."

"Okay. Apology accepted. Now can we talk about something else? How's the massage therapy with Wasabi coming along? Dad says he's improving daily." She kept her voice light, though the underlying tension in it was unmistakable.

Which made Shane reluctant to abide by her request. He wasn't ready to drop the subject.

"Remember that time in Albuquerque when I got thrown? You came running to my rescue then, too."

She gaped at him, proving she also remembered.

"Why did we stop dating, Cassidy?"

"I don't know. We were young and ambitious and both wanted championship titles."

She focused her attention on the children. The two reliable lesson mounts were placidly circling with their young passengers.

"We had a few good times," he said. "You and me."

"We did."

"I was jealous when you started dating Hoyt."

"Really?" Surprise flared in her eyes. "You never said anything."

"Maybe I should have."

Her eyes widened. "I didn't think you cared."

Shane nodded. Hoyt had been the better choice, or so he'd told himself.

"Do you miss competing?" he asked.

"Not at all. My life now is the arena and my son."

Had Hoyt's engagement so soon after he broke up with Cassidy hardened her heart? Shane didn't think so. Cassidy had been the one to end things. And she'd obviously dated other men. Pretty quickly after Hoyt, given she had a five-year-old son.

"If you don't mind my asking, what happened with you and Hoyt? One minute you were in love, the next you walked out on him."

"I do mind you asking."

"It's been a long time." What was the harm? Unless

she still cared about Hoyt. The thought didn't sit well with Shane for reasons he'd rather not examine.

"Exactly. It's been a long time and doesn't matter anymore." Grabbing the top fence railing, she placed her foot on the bottom one and hauled herself up. "Come on, Benjie. We really need to go."

Shane waited until she lowered herself to the ground before stating the obvious. "Every time I say something you don't like or that makes you uncomfortable, you run off."

He half expected her to deny it, but she didn't.

"Then stop saying things I don't like and that make me uncomfortable."

He chuckled and shook his head. "You're something else, Cassidy Beckett."

"I'll take *that* as a compliment."

"It was intended as one." More so than she probably realized.

She entered the pen and fetched her reluctant son. It seemed Benjie wasn't done playing with Bria. Shane was glad the two were getting along. He wanted his daughter to fit in at the Easy Money and to make friends.

"I supposed we should call it a day, too." He took hold of Skittles's bridle and led the horse through the gate. "I promised your mother I'd have you home by seven thirty."

Bria's features fell. "Can I stay over again?"

How he wished he could accommodate her. Nothing would make him happier. But he didn't dare push the boundaries of his agreement with Bria's mother, who'd been adamant that their daughter attend preschool on weekday mornings. Once he'd proved himself, then, yes, he'd insist on more time. Shane was smart enough to take things slowly.

"Sorry, kiddo. But maybe your mom will let you come back this weekend." Judy had mentioned attending a real estate class on Saturday. She might appreciate Shane babysitting.

While he and Cassidy unsaddled and brushed down the mounts, the kids played a game of tag in the barn aisle. Benjie could have easily won, but he let Bria catch him more than once.

"He's good with her," Shane told Cassidy. "Considering he's a year older and a boy."

"Benjie's used to socializing with kids of all ages. They're a staple at the arena." Untying Rusty's lead rope, she walked ahead. "Come on, Benjie. Help me put Rusty in his stall."

Bria stared after them, her expression bereft. Shane cheered her by lifting her up and setting her on Skittles's bare back.

"Hold on to his mane," he instructed and returned the old horse to his stall, three down from Rusty's. Shane used the opportunity to continue conversing with Cassidy.

"Maybe next Saturday we can take them on a trail ride together?" He'd heard a lot about the rolling mountains beyond the Easy Money's back pastures, but had not yet found the time to ride them.

"I'm working. The Jamboree's in two weeks."

She was referring to the arena's next big rodeo. Shane would be busy, too. Yet, he couldn't take no for an answer.

"How much would it hurt if we quit an hour early?" He removed Skittles's halter and lifted Bria from the horse's back. She scampered over to Benjie.

"I'm not going on a date with you," Cassidy said.

"It's not a date. We're talking a trail ride with Benjie and Bria. Invite your friend Tatum and her kids if you want."

"Bad idea." She shut the door on Rusty's stall. "Besides, I have other plans. A…family function."

"We were friends once. We can be again."

"It's complicated."

"Only if you make it complicated."

"No."

"Why? Because of Hoyt?"

"Of course not."

"You still care for him."

"I don't. He means nothing to me."

Shane recalled their brief kiss the other day and the sparks that had ignited between them. "What about me, Cassidy? Do I mean anything to you?"

Her sharp intake of breath and flustered denial should have been enough of an answer for him.

It wasn't, and Shane was more than prepared to see exactly how deep—or not—her feelings for him ran.

Chapter Four

Most women who owned SUVs did so because they had a pack of children to tote around. That was true for Cassidy and her friend Tatum. Cassidy didn't understand why her sister drove one. Liberty had always struck her as the consummate cowgirl, more comfortable behind the wheel of a pickup truck than anything else.

Yet, here they were, Cassidy, Liberty and their mother, heading into Mesa for a girls' afternoon, riding in style—*not*—in her sister's SUV. The vehicle was a mess. But instead of toys scattered across the floor of the back seat, there were a pair of old boots, a hoof pick, a bridle with a broken buckle, a spray bottle of mane detangler, bride magazines and an assortment of loose CDs.

The empty snack food wrappers, however, were the same as the ones in Cassidy's car. Literally, the same. Apparently, Liberty subscribed to a similar on-the-go diet as Benjie.

Cassidy rolled her eyes from her seat in the back. In the front, her mother and sister chatted nonstop about Liberty's wedding plans. They paid little attention to Cassidy, as long as she interjected the occasional comment about flowers or menu selections or veil versus no veil.

The wedding wasn't until the end of August—a date had finally been set—but, according to her mother and sister, the list of things to do in preparation was endless and required an eight-month head start.

In an attempt to chip away at the list, the three of them had taken off in the middle of what promised to be a slow day at the arena for some dress shopping and, if time allowed, a visit to the wedding supply store.

"Just to check out a few things," Liberty had said.

Right, Cassidy thought. *Define " few."*

Her father, brother and Tatum had volunteered to hold down the fort in their absence. Cassidy had wanted to stay behind, too, but her sister and mother wouldn't hear of it.

She relented after they agreed to include a stop at the party goods store. Benjie was turning six this coming weekend, and Cassidy was planning a party. Tatum's three kids and a half-dozen friends from school were coming. Benjie was beside himself with excitement.

"We're here," Liberty sang out, turning the SUV into the shopping center parking lot.

Cassidy tried to convince herself the sudden rush of nerves she suffered had nothing to do with wedding dress shopping and everything to do with the car that had swerved past them a little too close for comfort. Weddings in general made her uncomfortable. Perhaps because they all too often led to divorce.

They found a parking space right in front of Your-Special-Day.

"Kind of a silly name for a wedding shop." Cassidy slammed shut her door.

"You remember Valerie Kirkshaw's wedding last year?" Liberty marched ahead, speaking over her shoulder. "She bought her dress here. On sale. She swears this is the place to go."

Cassidy did remember the wedding and the dress. Both had been nice.

"She also said they have a huge selection of bridesmaid's dresses."

"Great." Cassidy mustered a smile as they entered the small, tastefully appointed shop. She might not be in the spirit of things, like her mother and sister, but neither would she ruin the day for them.

Thirty minutes sped by surprisingly fast. Liberty stood on a podium in the rear of the store, surrounded by mirrors and wearing her fourth dress. And, for the fourth time, Cassidy gawked in astonishment.

Her cowgirl sister, it seemed, had a penchant for very frilly, very fluffy, very girly wedding dresses, each one more stunning than the last.

Cassidy's mother circled Liberty, alternating between plucking at the voluminous folds and wiping away another tear. "You look beautiful, honey."

Indeed, she did. Cassidy's throat closed with emotion. She'd stopped dreaming of weddings years ago. On the day she'd walked away from Hoyt moments before telling him he was going to be a father. Then and there, she'd decided to dedicate her life to the baby growing inside her.

It wasn't as if guys ignored her. She'd been asked out, now and again. Usually by cowboys attending the rodeos. Less the last couple of years. She supposed, at thirty-five, she appealed less and less to the competitors, who seemed to be getting younger and younger each year. Perhaps her reputation for being standoffish preceded her.

She and Shane were nearly the same age, and he didn't think she was past her prime or standoffish. Not if the way his arms had tightened around her waist or the heat flared in his eyes were any indication.

That was new, she thought. He'd never looked at her like that before. If he had, they might have dated more than a few weeks. Then what?

"Cassidy. Your phone."

"Oh, yeah." At her mother's reminder, Cassidy roused herself and activated her phone's camera. It was her job to take a photo of each dress so Liberty could scrutinize them later. "Smile."

She snapped a picture, checking it to make sure it was in focus before taking a second and third from different angles.

Four more dresses were selected and tried on with the store clerk's help and guidance. Cassidy added notes to each picture, including pertinent details such as price and potential alterations.

"What do you have for bridesmaid dresses in pink?" Liberty asked, running her hand over the plastic garment cover of her favorite-thus-far dress.

"Pink!" Cassidy gasped, imagining the horrors ahead of her. "You said nothing about pink."

"It's a summer wedding. And the groomsmen are wearing dove grey tuxes."

"But pink?" Who was this woman impersonating her sister and where had she hidden Liberty?

"Weren't you listening in the car on the way over?"

No, she hadn't been.

"Might I suggest a pale rose instead?" the clerk said. "It's perfect for August."

Rose had a better ring to it than pink.

The clerk showed them to the racks holding bridesmaid dresses, arranged by style and color.

"Oh, look at this one." Her mother held up a tea-length creation trimmed with a delicate lace.

Liberty rushed forward. "I love it!"

Cassidy let out an expansive sigh.

While Liberty waited, seated on a velveteen upholstered chair with a seashell-shaped back, the clerk fawned over her. Cassidy and her mother ventured into the dressing room, six rose-colored dresses held high so as not to drag on the floor.

Sliding into the first one, Cassidy waited for her mother to zip her up. When that didn't happen, she asked, "Something stuck?"

"No." Her mother sniffed.

Cassidy turned around, holding the narrow straps of the dress to keep them from falling. "What's wrong, Mom?"

"I'm fine. Just a bit emotional." Her mother's smile wobbled. "It's a big deal when your daughter marries."

Cassidy supposed it was. Feeling a little emotional herself, she patted her mother's arm. "Hang in there, Mom."

"I thought you'd be the first."

Cassidy managed an awkward shrug, the dress still gaping in the back. "Hoyt and I never discussed the M word."

"You ever think what might have happened if you'd tracked him down sooner? Before he met his wife."

"Sure. In the beginning. But I doubt I would have married him."

"Because he liked to drink?"

"Drink *and* drive. Let's not forget that."

Growing up with an alcoholic father—former alcoholic, the rest of her family was quick to point out—Cassidy had little tolerance for people who imbibed to excess. She particularly had no tolerance for people who then got behind the wheel of a vehicle, as her father had the night he drove his truck into the well house with Cassidy in the front passenger seat.

Finally, her mother zipped up the dress, enclosing Cassidy inside layers upon layers of rose taffeta. "Shane doesn't drink."

"And why should that matter to me?"

"I've seen him watching you."

Cassidy tugged on the sides of the dress, adjusting the fit. "He's just curious is all. I did once date his brother."

"More than date him. You two had a ch—"

"Mom, not here," Cassidy said in a terse whisper.

"It could explain Shane's curiosity."

"You think he suspects?" Breathing became difficult. The dress's snug bodice could be responsible. More likely it was her constant anxiety.

"Or he likes you. In that way."

Cassidy's anxiety increased.

She stared at herself in the mirror, not quite seeing her reflection. What bothered her most wasn't that Shane might like her. It was that she might like him back. Yes, in that way.

Liberty hailed them from the dressing room entrance. "What's taking so long, you two?"

"Be right there." Cassidy's mother pushed open the double swinging doors after giving Cassidy a final inspection. "You're stunning. No one could blame Shane."

Cassidy walked out to show her sister, a slight unsteadiness to her legs. She'd hardly reached the podium when her sister snapped a picture with her phone.

No decisions were made. Liberty wanted to visit another shop or two first. Cassidy was admittedly relieved and glad when they pulled into the arena driveway two hours later. She alone had packages to unload, having made a haul for Benjie's birthday at the party supply store.

Leaving the bags on the kitchen table, she headed straight for the arena. School had let out thirty minutes ago, and the students participating in the afternoon riding program would arrive any second. While Liberty was in charge, Cassidy frequently helped with the advanced students.

Doc Worthington's familiar truck was parked near the bull pens. He, her father and Shane emerged from behind the chutes. Cassidy's route forced her to either meet up with them or make an obvious and rude detour. Reluctantly, she chose the former.

"Good news." Her father beamed. "Doc here thinks Wasabi's coming along and will be ready to compete in the Jamboree next weekend."

Feeling the intensity of Shane's gaze on her, she struggled to remain focused on her father. "That is good news."

"Shane's done a right fine job." Doc Worthington's low laugh sounded like an engine rumbling to life on a cold morning. "Who'd've guessed. Massage therapy on a bull. What'll they think of next?"

"Don't know until you try." Shane's tone and smile were both humble. And endearing.

Cassidy was undeniably affected.

Spying several cars pulling into the parking area, she said, "Excuse me. I have a class to teach."

Before she managed a single step, Benjie charged out from behind a parked horse trailer, legs churning and arms swinging.

"Mom! Mom!" He stopped in front of her, red-faced and short of breath. "Did you get the invitations?"

"Yes, sweetie, they're on the kitchen table."

"It's my birthday on Friday," he announced to the group. "But we're having the party Saturday. So more kids can come."

Doc Worthington gave him a pat on his head. "How old will you be?"

"Six."

"Six, huh?" Shane said. "I thought you might be seven. Seeing as how big you are."

Benjie puffed up, adding an extra inch to his height. "I'm the third oldest in my class."

Cassidy fought the surge of panic building inside her. This was exactly the reason she hadn't mentioned Benjie's birthday to Shane earlier. If he bothered to count backward, he might realize she and his brother had been dating at the time she'd gotten pregnant. Though it had been in the last days of their relationship. Right before their big fight. She hadn't noticed her missed period until three weeks after their breakup.

Did guys think about things like when conception occurred? She risked a quick peek at Shane from beneath lowered lids. He didn't appear to be counting backward in his head. Rather, he was smiling pleasantly as Benjie rambled on about the party.

"We're gonna have pony rides and birthday cake and a piñata."

"Sounds like a good time."

"Can Bria come?" Benjie asked.

"I'll see. Thanks for the invitation." He turned to Cassidy. "If your mom doesn't mind."

She could hardly say no. Nor would she. "Of course. Bria's more than welcome."

Doc Worthington made a show of taking out his invoice pad and pen. "Hate to leave, but I've got another appointment."

Cassidy's father got the hint. "Let me get you paid for today."

The two men beelined for the office.

"Grandpa, can I come, too?" Benjie hurried after them, leaving Cassidy and Shane alone.

She could have called her son back, but didn't. When Shane moved closer, and the inevitable hum coursed through her, she reconsidered.

"You don't have to invite Bria," he said. "I can give Benjie some excuse."

"Nonsense. I should have thought of inviting her myself."

"All right." His mouth curved at the corners.

To her chagrin, her defenses crumbled. He did have the sexiest smile she'd ever seen.

"We accept."

We? She blinked at his use of the plural. What had she been thinking? Or not thinking. Naturally, he'd come with his daughter. At least to drop her off and pick her up. Only "we accept" sounded like he intended to stay for the duration of the party.

"Great. I'll, ah, have Benjie leave an invitation at the trailer with the details."

"Looking forward to it."

Cassidy headed to the arena gate to meet her sister, acutely aware of Shane watching her every step of the way.

"You okay?" Liberty asked, concern filling her eyes. "You look a little flushed."

Was that all? Her cheeks felt like they were on fire.

"I DON'T KNOW, SHANE. Seems like a lot of driving for you to do in one day."

"I don't mind."

There was a pause on the phone as Judy considered his request to take Bria for an unscheduled visit tomorrow. "You'd have to be here early in the morning. By seven sharp. My class starts at eight."

"No problem."

"And have her home by six. It's pizza night."

"No problem."

Another pause. Judy wasn't making this easy on him. Their agreement as to when and for how long he had their daughter was literally brand-new and on a trial basis. He didn't want to pressure Judy too much or not keep his word, just on the chance she'd react negatively.

On the other hand, someone had to watch Bria while Judy attended her all-day real estate class. Why not Shane instead of the sweet, elderly neighbor? Especially when he could take Bria to a birthday party with other children her age. A much better option than her sitting in front of a TV for hours on end. Shane hadn't included that last part when he made his pitch to Judy.

He heard a long, drawn-out sigh. He also heard a man's voice in the background, muffled and indistinguishable. Must be the fiancé, Shane thought, and ground his teeth. Was the man telling her not to give in?

"Fine," Judy finally said. "See you in the morning."

"Thanks. I appreciate it."

Shane was grateful for Judy's understanding, and from what he could tell, her fiancé's cooperation. Perhaps he'd jumped to the wrong conclusion and the three of them *could* effectively parent Bria.

Pocketing his phone, Shane continued walking down Center Avenue, Reckless's main thoroughfare. Normally, he'd be at the arena on a Friday afternoon. Mercer, however, had cut him and several of the bull wranglers loose for the evening.

With the Jamboree Rodeo just next weekend, practicing for events was at an all-time frenzy. A group of calf ropers had reserved the arena tonight, under Cassidy's direction, which meant there would be no bull-riding practices until tomorrow. Shane had decided to take advantage of the unexpected free time by familiarizing himself with the town and, now that he and Bria were officially attending Benjie's birthday party, shop for a gift.

What did one get a six-year-old boy? All Shane and his brother had wanted at Benjie's age were things related to do horses and riding. Living at the Easy Money Arena, Benjie already had more than Shane could have ever dreamed of owning.

He crossed at the next corner, taking in the sights. Reckless boasted the usual small-town businesses: feed store, gas station, several restaurants, ice cream parlor, convenience market that also rented DVDs and sold bait, a shipping store, two real estate offices, a post office and public library.

In addition, there was a multitude of shops catering to tourists, the town's main industry next to the Easy Money Arena. Those included a bookstore with offerings by local authors in the window, a novelty shop, a photo studio specializing in old-time photographs, two jewelry stores and three antique shops.

Shane was just thinking there was nothing in any of the shops or stores of interest to Benjie, and a trip to nearby Globe was probably in order, when he happened to pass the Silver Dollar Pawn Shop. There in the window was a set of shiny golf clubs. Of course Benjie didn't play golf, but the clubs gave Shane an idea, and he went inside.

"Afternoon." The woman behind the counter flashed him a ready smile that scattered the many wrinkles on her face in different directions. Her gray hair was so tightly permed, it sat upon her head like a knit ski cap. "Holler if you need help."

"Do you by chance carry sports equipment?"

"Some. Over this way." She emerged from behind the counter. It was then Shane noticed she was maybe four-eleven at most, even with her bright pink sneakers. "What kind of equipment did you have in mind?"

"Football. Baseball. Basketball. Something for a young kid."

"Everything I have is right here." She guided him to the last aisle where golf clubs, tennis rackets, ice skates and, Shane was pleased to see, football, baseball and basketball equipment, some of it in decent shape, lined the shelves. "There's a selection of autographed memorabilia in the case over there."

Shane gave the case a cursory once-over. "Not sure memorabilia is what I need."

The woman's smile didn't as much as flicker. "What are you looking for?"

Shane pushed back his cowboy hat and scratched behind his ear. "The thing is, I'm not sure if the kid likes sports. I just figured, he's a boy and most boys do."

"That's a fact. This boy a relation of yours?"

"My boss's grandson. I work for the Becketts."

She snapped her fingers. "You're that new bull manager they hired."

"Guilty as charged." Shane wasn't surprised she'd heard of him, what with Reckless being a typical small town and the Becketts its most prominent residents.

"The boy you're talking about must be Cassidy's youngster, Benjie. My granddaughter's going to his party."

This was promising. "Any suggestions on what might interest him?"

"From what DeAnna tells me, he's quite the class clown."

"I've heard that, too."

"She hasn't mentioned sports, but as you say, he's a boy. And he doesn't have a father around to play any with him."

The woman could be considered by some to be a gossip. Shane thought she was simply making small talk. He hadn't been at the Easy Money long, yet he, too, had already figured out there was no father in Benjie's life.

"Cassidy does her best," the woman continued as Shane scrutinized the array of sports equipment. "Works her tail off to provide for her son."

Shane had observed the same thing and admired her for it. He might be new to parenthood, but he'd quickly realized raising a child required tremendous sacrifice and dedication.

He selected a Rawlings outfield baseball glove that appeared to be in mint condition. Turning it over in his hands, he noted the logo, size and price tag still attached by a plastic string.

"The man who brought it in claimed it's brand-new," the woman said.

"Seems to be." Shane fingered the dangling price tag.

The glove was probably a little too large for Benjie. Better than too small, Shane reasoned. Room to grow.

Sports had played a large part in Shane's high school days. He'd made the varsity football and baseball teams when he was just a sophomore. During his senior year, he quit school sports to focus exclusively on rodeo. The decision paid off, launching him on a career that would become his life and give him a marketable trade.

"There's a bat by the same manufacturer." The woman indicated a rack at the end of the aisle, the bats in it standing upright, as if at attention.

Shane lifted the solid wood Rawlings bat, testing the weight in his hand. Not too heavy, not too light. Like the glove, it appeared barely used.

While part of him worried he wasn't buying Benjie something brand-new and fresh from the factory, a high-quality glove and bat would make a fine gift. He was actually more worried Benjie wouldn't like them.

"You're going to need a ball to go with those," the woman said. "You take all three, and I'll cut you a deal."

A few minutes later, Shane stood at the counter, removing his bank card from his wallet as the woman bagged his purchases.

"Hard to believe that boy of Cassidy's is six already." The woman passed the bag across the counter, then accepted Shane's card and ran it through the scanner. "I remember when she quit the rodeo circuit and came home to have him. Seems like it was yesterday."

"Time flies." Shane was thinking of his daughter, Bria, and all the years he'd missed with her.

Not a day passed he didn't count his blessings. Had Judy kept Bria from him, he could have wound up like Mercer, going twenty-five years before learning he'd fathered a daughter.

"We all figured at some point her boyfriend would step up and claim the boy. Didn't happen. Guess he's not interested."

"His loss." Again, Shane thought of Bria and the day she came into his life.

The woman escorted him to the door. "Nice to meet you, Shane. Enjoy the party."

"I will. Thanks."

"Be sure and come back."

"Count on it."

He returned to his truck and tossed the bag onto the passenger seat before getting in. He was debating checking out the pizza parlor when something the woman said came back to him. This time, he paid attention.

We all figured at some point her boyfriend would step up and claim the boy. Didn't happen. Guess he's not interested.

Six years ago. Shane remembered it well. He'd recently won his second world bull-riding championship in December at the National Finals Rodeo. He'd taken the month of January off to recuperate from his injuries. The gal he'd been dating at the time, also a barrel racer, was friends with Cassidy.

The gal had sat on the end of the couch where he was resting, his left ankle elevated atop a stack of pillows, and announced that Cassidy had just given birth to a boy.

"A couple weeks sooner," she had said, "and her baby could've been Hoyt's."

Shane hadn't thought much about it at the time. In part, because his brain was fuzzy due to pain meds. Also, his brother was engaged and soon to be married.

Now, though, Shane did give it consideration. What was the old saying? There were no such things as coincidences.

Was Benjie his brother's son? Did he dare ask Cassidy? More importantly, did he say anything to Hoyt? If Benjie were his son, he'd want to know. He'd *insist* on knowing.

Despite a former lifestyle many people considered wild and impulsive, Shane never moved forward without careful thought and consideration. To that end, he placed a call to Hoyt.

"Hey, buddy!" His brother's greeting was exuberant. "How's it going?"

Shane sat in his truck, out of the cool weather and sheltered from the wind that had kicked up earlier, and chatted with Hoyt for several minutes, filling him in on how things were progressing with the new job.

"I'll be in Payson next month," Hoyt said. "Why don't you drive up to meet me?"

"I just might take you up on that." Shane couldn't think of a way to casually break the ice, so he just went for it. "You know, Cassidy's here in Reckless."

There was the briefest of pauses. Any number of reasons could have accounted for it. Shane didn't jump to conclusions.

"How's she doing?" Hoyt asked.

Prettier than ever, Shane thought. Stubborn, bristly at times, fiercely independent, sexy as hell, infuriating, but in a way that made him want to take her in his arms and kiss her till she melted.

He didn't tell his brother any of those things. "She's good."

"Glad to hear it."

"When was it you two broke up?"

"Jeez, I don't remember. Six, seven years ago. It was right after the Down Home Days Rodeo. Spring, I guess."

Shane had competed in the Down Home Days Rodeo enough times to know it fell in April. If Cassidy had gotten together with another man, it had either been immediately after she'd broken up with Hoyt or she'd cheated on him.

There was a third scenario, and it was making more and more sense by the minute. Hoyt had fathered a son and didn't have the slightest idea.

"Guess I forgot how long it's been," Shane said matter-of-factly. After a few more minutes of catching up with his brother, he ended the call with, "Talk to you next week."

Leaning back against the truck seat, he eyed the bag with the baseball equipment. Without knowing for sure, or, at least having more to go on than an inkling, Shane wouldn't voice his suspicions about Benjie to Hoyt. First, he needed to talk to Cassidy. Then, he'd decide on his next step.

Chapter Five

Benjie, usually a handful, was in rare form for his birthday party. When he wasn't tearing around the backyard, seeing what kind of trouble he could stir up, he was yelling at the top of his lungs and commanding attention. Cassidy bit back another warning and told herself not to stress. This was his birthday, after all. And most of the other children were also being handfuls, though to lesser degrees.

None of the adults seemed to mind too much. His grandparents shamelessly indulged Benjie, accommodating his every wish. His aunt Liberty and future uncle, Deacon, declared he and his little friends were "just being kids." His uncle Ryder filmed the entire party with his digital camcorder, capturing the pony relay races, a rousing game of kick ball and breaking open the candy-filled piñata. Cassidy's best friend, Tatum, helped out wherever and whenever an extra pair of hands was needed.

Cassidy's mother gleefully finished serving cake and ice cream to the last of the children. Cassidy grimaced. Great, just what they needed. More sugar to fuel their already over-the-top energy levels.

Benjie bounded up to her, cake crumbs and blue frosting smeared over his face. "Can we open presents now?"

"In a bit."

Rather than argue with her, which is what she expected,

he ran straight for Shane, his new best buddy. The two of them had been practically inseparable the entire party. Before Benjie caused a collision, Shane scooped up the boy and swung him in a circle.

"Me next," one of the other children shouted, and Shane obliged.

He'd been wonderful the entire party. Arriving early with his daughter, he'd set up the tables and chairs, readied Skittles and the other horses for the relay race and kept Benjie occupied and out from underfoot. The latter might account for their bonding.

Or, Cassidy fretted, was it something intangible? Did they have a connection because they were related, though neither of them knew it?

Since separating them was impossible, she did the next best thing by constantly putting herself in their immediate vicinity. That way, she could monitor them, though hearing their exchanges left her just as rattled as not hearing them.

"Daddy!" Bria dragged a little girl by the hand to where Shane played with the boys. Cassidy recognized the girl as the granddaughter of Mrs. Danelli, the owner of the Silver Dollar Pawn Shop. The little girl was also Benjie's classmate at school. "DeAnna invited me to spend the night at her house."

Shane set down the boy "passenger" he'd been giving an "airplane" ride. "Can't, honey. I told your mom I'd have you home by six tonight."

"No, next weekend, Daddy."

"We have the rodeo."

Cassidy had heard from her father that, because Bria would be at the Easy Money for her regular visit, he was giving Shane more time off than normal during the rodeo. The only thing her father had insisted on was Shane be available during the bull-riding events.

Cassidy didn't know who Shane had recruited to watch his daughter, if anyone. She herself had hired one of her teenaged riding students to babysit Benjie. Should she offer the girl's services to Shane? Cassidy couldn't decide.

"DeAnna's coming to the rodeo, too," Bria told her father.

Her new friend confirmed with a shy nod of her head.

"Well," Shane hedged. "Let me talk to DeAnna's mother when she comes to pick her up."

The girls seemed satisfied for the moment and scampered off, cute as could be.

"Do you know this girl's mother?"

Realizing Shane was speaking to her, Cassidy spun to face him. "A little. We've met at some school functions. She's nice."

"Is she responsible?"

Cassidy almost laughed. In her experience dealing with parents at the arena, the question was one she'd expect from another mother, not a father. "I'd say yes. However, I'm basing that solely on our discussion when I delivered DeAnna's invitation. She made sure the party would be well supervised before accepting. That struck me as responsible."

"Will you talk to her with me? I'm still pretty new at this." Shane looked chagrined.

Cassidy felt herself warming to him. Then again, all he had to do was flash his amazing smile and she warmed from head to toe.

"Why don't you stop by her house first? You'll be able to get a feel for her parenting skills just from looking around."

He hesitated. "Won't she be offended?"

"It's a reasonable request," she assured him. "But if you're uncomfortable with being so forthright, suggest you need to discuss the sleepover first before agreeing. If she refuses, then you have your answer."

"Good idea."

Cassidy met his gaze, and the intensity of it rendered her momentarily mute. He'd had that kind of effect on her ever since his return. What was different now?

"Thanks for helping out today," she finally managed. "I do appreciate it."

"Happy to."

"I know Benjie appreciates it, too."

"He's a great kid. It's a shame his father can't be here."

Cassidy instantly froze. Though this was hardly the first comment about Hoyt she'd had to deflect, this was the first comment from his brother. And, either her imagination was running amok or there was an odd quality in Shane's tone.

Collecting her scattered wits, she said, "He couldn't be here. He lives...out of state."

"Where?"

"I beg your pardon?"

"Where? What state?"

She resisted telling him it was none of his damn business. "Um, last I heard, Ohio. He moves around a lot."

"Because of his work?"

"Yes."

So much for putting herself in Shane's vicinity. Big mistake. She couldn't flee fast enough. "If you'll excuse me, I told Benjie he could open his presents."

Shane didn't let her go two feet before falling into step beside her. "I'll round up the kids."

"You've done so much already."

"I like your family, especially Benjie." His voice lowered and turned a shade huskier. "I like you, too. You can't say you haven't noticed."

Good grief! Had anyone heard him? She swore silently

when she caught Liberty's eagle eye zeroing in on them. All hope they'd escaped notice was dashed when Liberty winked, pointed at Shane behind the shield of her hand and mouthed, "I approve."

If her sister knew the truth, that Shane was actually Benjie's uncle, would she still be supportive of the match? Liberty had been denied knowing her real father until she was twenty-four years old. Cassidy was doing much the same thing to her own son.

She doubted Liberty would be supportive or understanding. Especially since Cassidy had lied to everyone except their mother, telling them Benjie's father wanted nothing to do with his son.

In fact, should the truth ever come out, it could tear the Becketts further apart, undoing all the progress they'd made these past six months.

Her decision had seemed so simple at the time. Not endangering Hoyt's upcoming marriage by dropping a bombshell at the last minute. Avoiding being a home wrecker for the second time. Sparing herself the same heartache her mother had endured should Benjie one day choose to leave Reckless and live with his father.

Except everything hung by a flimsy thread that was threatening to snap any second.

"Benjie," Cassidy called, then said to Shane, "I've got to go."

To her consternation, he followed her to the back porch where the presents lay stacked in the middle of a picnic table. Benjie was already there with his buddies, each of them pushing and shoving for a closer glimpse of his birthday booty. The girls practiced considerably more decorum.

"You sit here, young man," she instructed, giving his shoulder a light nudge.

He obliged, but not before grabbing a present. No

sooner was he seated than he attacked the wrapping paper. Ryder was there with the camcorder, filming every minute of her son's greedy antics. The rest of the family gathered around, watching over the heads of the children, each of whom wanted the guest of honor to open their present first.

"Wait," Cassidy admonished. "Read the card first." Did her son not have any manners?

Benjie stopped long enough to discover this gift was from Tatum's children.

"What do you say?"

"Thank you." Benjie barely got the words out before resuming his assault on the wrapping paper. "Yes!" His eyes lit up. "A remote control car." His second thank-you was considerably more sincere.

It continued like that for several more gifts. Then Benjie grabbed a gunny sack, the contents weighing it down.

"There's no card," he lamented after looking the sack over, his features forming a puzzled frown. "Is this a present?"

"Sorry," Shane apologized. "I'm not much for gift wrapping."

Benjie laughed and untied the sack, then peered inside, his mouth falling open. "It's a baseball bat! And a glove." He gazed at Shane with a mixture of astonishment and pure joy. "Thanks, Mister Shane."

"There's a ball in there, too. It probably fell to the bottom."

Benjie discarded the sack in favor of balancing this newest treasure on his lap. "Look, Mom." His buddies crowded around him, admiring the gift and expressing their envy.

"I see," Cassidy said, a lump in the back of her throat taking her by surprise.

"Just what I wanted."

Did he? She supposed he'd asked for sports equipment before, but she couldn't remember. Or was it that she didn't put much importance on non-horse sports? The kind of sports a father and son might share.

Until six months ago, when Cassidy's father returned to Reckless, her son had had no male figures in his life other than the wranglers at the ranch. Now, besides his grandfather, he had Cassidy's brother, Ryder and, she swallowed in an attempt to dislodge the lump, Shane. His other uncle.

Shane hadn't been here two weeks, and he'd already figured out what her son wanted most. What he needed. Baseball equipment.

"Will you play with me later?" Benjie asked Shane, his features alight with hope.

"You bet."

The rest of the present unwrapping was a blur for Cassidy. She busied herself organizing the cards so Benjie could write thank-you notes. Shane hadn't included a card. Something told her she wouldn't need it to prod her memory.

He stood in front of her as if she'd conjured him with her thoughts. "Let me." Without waiting for an answer, he relieved her of the packages she'd gathered to carry into the house.

She sighed, too physically, emotionally and mentally tired from the long afternoon to object. She'd barely organized a second load when he returned.

"I put the presents in the living room. On the couch."

"Great."

This time when he carried the presents into the house, she accompanied him, bringing a large plastic bag filled with trash. As they entered the kitchen, Benjie and Bria passed them, tripping over their feet in their haste.

"Slow down," Cassidy cautioned.

"Where are you two heading?" Shane asked.

Benjie stopped long enough to wave a package of batteries. "Grandma gave these to me for my remote control car. I'm gonna show Bria how it works."

His cousin, Cassidy just then realized. And they got along as if they'd grown up together.

The door hadn't quite shut when she heard Benjie say to Bria, "You're lucky. I wish I had a dad like yours."

Earlier, when Shane commented on Benjie's father not being at the party, Cassidy had frozen in place. This time, she turned hot all over, as if she was standing in front of a roaring bonfire. Worse, when she dared glance up, she found Shane observing her with unwavering concentration. Awareness flickered in his eyes.

He knows.

She dismissed the notion. He didn't know. He couldn't. She'd been too careful all these years. It had to be something else.

"I suppose we should get back to the party."

Shane didn't move. "Wait, Cassidy. There's something I need to ask you."

"Now?" She steadied herself. "I'm kind of busy."

"This can't wait."

"It'll have to," she said walked away.

His next words stopped her short of the door and nearly knocked her to her knees.

"Is Hoyt Benjie's father?"

SHANE HAD TO give Cassidy credit. Once the initial shock wore off, she pulled herself together and acted as though he'd asked about her dinner plans and not if Hoyt was her son's father.

Was he wrong about his suspicions, or was she well practiced in the art of deception? He intended to find out. Leading her outside, he took her to a far corner of the yard.

"Daddy, where you going?" Bria chased after them,

her sweater buttoned crookedly and her purple barrettes coming loose from her hair.

"We'll be right back, honey."

"But DeAnna's mom is coming. You said you'd talk to her."

He hesitated. He had promised to speak to DeAnna's mother about the possible sleepover next weekend.

"I won't be long."

"Can I come with you?"

"We can do this later," Cassidy said, offering a weak smile.

Shane wasn't going to let her get off easily. Their conversation was too important. All of their futures depended on it.

"Wait here, Bria," he told his daughter. "Watch for DeAnna's mother and come get me when she arrives, okay?"

Bria pouted. The next instant, she brightened when her new friend insisted she join in a game of tag.

"You're wasting your time," Cassidy said. "Hoyt's not Benjie's father."

She didn't take her eyes off the group of kids, one of whom was Benjie. He stood out from the rest, because of his height and exuberant nature.

Hoyt was like that. Taller than average and with a gregarious personality.

"Humor me." Shane chose a spot behind the modular play set. Earlier, it had served as an imaginary fort for a trio of boys.

Cassidy faced him calmly, her sole sign of any turmoil a thin layer of perspiration dotting her brow.

"Please don't be angry," he said. "But I need you to be honest with me. Are you sure Hoyt isn't Benjie's father?"

"*You* need me?"

"For Hoyt's sake."

"Besides the fact it's none of your business, why would

you even think that?" She stuffed her hands in her jacket pockets.

"He's turning six. I can count. At least up to eight."

Cassidy glared at him. Clearly, his joke about how long a competitor needed to remain on a bull in order to qualify didn't strike her as funny.

"You have to admit, the timing is right."

"Don't you think if he was Hoyt's son, I'd have told him?"

"To be honest, I'm not sure."

"What reason would I have to lie?"

Another non-answer. She was good at giving them.

"Are you willing to let Benjie take a DNA test?"

The color drained from her face. "I'm not subjecting him to any test."

"Because you're afraid of the results?"

"We're done talking about this." She spoke through gritted teeth. "Don't ever bring it up again."

"How about I bring it up with Hoyt?" He reached for his cell phone in the front pocket of his vest. "Right now."

She gasped. "You wouldn't."

Shane hated being so hard on her, but he'd gone four years having no idea he was a father. He couldn't stand idly by and let the same thing happen to his brother. Especially when Hoyt wanted children and would be a good father. Cassidy had no right to deny him. And putting off questioning her would give her time to throw up more barriers. Possibly leave town with Benjie.

"I'm sorry, Cassidy. But unless you give me the name of Benjie's father, I refuse to drop this."

"I repeat, this is none of your business."

"It's very much my business if Benjie is my nephew."

"I'm not giving you the name of his father. So you can do what? Call and confront him?"

"You said he knows about Benjie and doesn't want any part of him."

"If you don't quit badgering me this instant, I'm going to talk to my parents."

Nothing she said or did would change Shane's mind. This was a mother fiercely protecting her child from what she perceived as a threat. If Hoyt weren't Benjie's father, she'd have no reason to react so defensively.

"And tell them what?" He met her angry glare head-on, not the least bit intimidated. "You're upset because I'm asking a reasonable question? Your father didn't know about Liberty until six months ago. Do you seriously think he'll support you hiding Benjie from my brother?"

"Stop staying that!" Her glance darted wildly about. "Someone might hear you."

"No one can hear." Indeed, the party had thinned considerably. Most of the children were gone and, with the exception of Sunny and Mercer, all of the adult family members, too. Luckily for Shane, DeAnna's mother was late. He still had time to call Cassidy's bluff and dialed Hoyt's number.

"Please." She closed her eyes. "Don't do this."

Shane thought of demanding the name of Benjie's father again. Her fragile state stopped him. Instead, he softened his voice and attempted to explain.

"Five years ago, I was a different person. Unsettled. A bit crazy. Okay, a lot crazy," he amended when she sent him a look. "Some folks said I was hell-bent on killing myself, and, well, I almost did. I can understand why Judy assumed I wouldn't make a good father. That didn't, however, justify her hiding her pregnancy. I had a right to be part of Bria's life. To help raise her if I wanted. Who's to say how I would have reacted if I'd known? I might have quit rodeoing then and there."

"Do you truly believe that? You wouldn't have won your last world championship title."

"The thing is, we'll never know for sure."

Tears welled in Cassidy's eyes. "It's different for you. Judy and Bria live in Mesa. Not far from Reckless."

"Because I moved here. When I retired from the circuit, I searched for a job that would put me close to them. It was my good fortune your father happened to be looking for a bull manager."

"Benjie's father lives in another state."

Right. What had she told him? Ohio? "That's still no reason. He could relocate." Would Hoyt move? He and his wife had just bought a new house. "Or visit. And Benjie could visit him."

Her angry reaction took him aback. "Not happening," she bit out. "Not ever."

"Cassidy. There's more than you to consider here. There's the father *and* Benjie."

She shook her head. "My brother left when he was fourteen to live with our father. We hardly saw him after that. Broke my mother's heart and mine."

"The reasons were different. Ryder and your mother were at odds."

"You don't know about my family."

"I know a little. Ryder told me the circumstances. How you and he also fought about your father."

She stiffened.

"He also told me he regrets not spending more time with you and Liberty. Is that what you want for Benjie? To miss out on having a father in his life?"

"It didn't hurt me any."

Shane laid a hand on Cassidy's shoulder. "I disagree. You're hurting right now."

The slight tremors he felt beneath his hand confirmed it. As did the shaky breath she drew.

"I won't lose Benjie. He's all I have."

"Who's to say you will lose him?"

"What if he tries to take him away?"

He. For the first time, she hadn't used the ambiguous term *Benjie's father.* Not exactly an admission, but close.

"He won't. You're a good mother, Cassidy. A great mother. The most he'll get is visitation."

"I could lose Benjie all summer."

"Think of what he gets in return. A father who can contribute financially. Improve the quality of his life."

She bristled. "I support my son just fine."

"No one's saying you don't. But think of how much more he can have with Hoyt contributing." Shane continued to press. "My brother's not a bad guy. He'll be good to Benjie. Spend time with him. Teach him. Introduce him to our family. Our parents."

Several seconds passed without Cassidy saying a word. Shane was mentally patting himself on the back for getting through to her when she turned the tables on him.

"I'm asking you to respect my wishes and not say anything to Hoyt."

"What if I don't?"

"It's not your place." She enunciated each word.

"I can help you tell him, if you want."

"You don't understand."

"Make me understand."

"You're thinking only of Hoyt. What about Benjie? His entire life could be changed. Disrupted. He may not be ready."

Shane shook his head. "You're making excuses. He wants a father. You heard him."

"How dare you spring this on me? At my son's birthday party of all places. You threaten me and expect me to go along simply because you happen to think you're right based solely on your own experience."

Had he threatened her? He could see how she might feel that way. He had come on strong.

Against his better judgment, he relented. "Okay."

She stared at him with tear-filled eyes. "Okay what?"

"I won't tell Hoyt."

"Thank you." Her breath left her body in a rush.

"Don't thank me yet. I won't tell Hoyt because you're the one who will."

"I just said I won't."

"I'm going to convince you otherwise, Cassidy. And to warn you, I'll be relentless."

Bria came running, shouting that DeAnna's mother had arrived, which spared Cassidy from having to respond.

Shane was too smart to think she didn't have more to say on the subject. Once she recovered from the shock, he was no doubt in for an earful. From what he knew about Ms. Beckett, she could be every bit as relentless as he was. Possibly more.

Chapter Six

Cassidy slipped into the tack room on the pretense of fetching a replacement brow band for one of the barrel racer's bridles. The truth was, she desperately needed a few minutes alone to get herself under control. This past week, she'd staved off the beginnings of a panic attack at least a dozen times. Three times just today, including now. Rather than risk someone noticing her usual behavior and asking questions, she'd ducked into the tack room.

The one problem was her odd behavior had been noticed. Especially by Shane, who, not an hour ago, inquired if she was all right.

Slumping against the wall, she inhaled slowly and deeply, the familiar scent of leather and oil filling her nostrils and easing her tension. Marginally. Every moment she didn't completely immerse herself in a task, she was recalling her conversation with Shane. He'd promised not to tell Hoyt about Benjie and, so far, he'd kept his promise.

He'd also kept his promise about attempting to change her mind, and their constant conversations were draining her emotionally and mentally.

Another wave of anxiety struck. Cassidy couldn't be more afraid if she was pinned in the path of an oncoming vehicle.

She'd suffered similar bouts when she was ten, after

the accident when her father had driven the truck carrying them both into the well house. Rather than disappearing after he left, they'd worsened. So much so, her mother had finally taken Cassidy to see a doctor.

Eventually, and with the help of counseling, the anxiety disappeared. Until this past week.

Cassidy buried her face in her hands. She couldn't go on like this. Not for much longer. Complaining to her parents would do no good. If they fired Shane and sent him away, he might, and probably would, tell Hoyt about Benjie.

What if she went to Shane? Pleaded with him again not to reveal her secret. She scoffed. He wouldn't agree. She could still hear him talking about Bria and how the girl's mother had kept her from him all those years.

Her only choice was to tell Hoyt and pray he'd be one of those loser fathers who didn't give a flying fig about their offspring. Instinct told her that wasn't going to be the case. Hoyt wanted children. According to Shane, he and his wife were actively trying for one of their own and having no luck.

They would probably jump all over the chance at seeing Benjie. Getting to know him. Taking him for visits. Seeking custody.

Cassidy's heart twisted inside her chest, pressing painfully into her sternum. The next instant, a bright light flashed in her face, causing her to flinch and shield her face.

"Hey, what are you doing in here?"

The voice belonged to Tatum.

Cassidy blinked, bringing her friend into focus. "Just needed a few minutes alone."

"In the dark?"

"I thought the bulb was burned out."

Tatum moved closer, concern written over her lovely oval face. "What's wrong?"

For days—actually since the moment she'd heard her father had hired Shane for the bull manager position—Cassidy had been carrying a heavy weight. Like an anvil hanging from a chain around her neck. She wanted nothing more than to unburden herself.

"Where do I start?" With that, Cassidy broke into sobs.

Immediately, her friend engulfed her in a soothing embrace. "Oh, honey. How can I help you?"

Cassidy allowed herself a good cry and, when it was over, admitted she felt better. Fortunately, no one had come looking for either her or Tatum.

"Let's get out of here," her friend suggested, and led Cassidy across the barn aisle to the empty office. "Your mom's busy setting up the registration booth for tomorrow morning. We have the place to ourselves." Just to be sure, she put the Be Back Soon sign in the window and locked both doors.

Cassidy helped herself to a cup of water from the cooler then dropped into a visitor chair. Tatum wheeled her chair from behind her desk and positioned it next to Cassidy's, then folded Cassidy's hand in hers.

"Tell me," she coaxed.

The two of them had been friends since elementary school. It was easy for Cassidy to pour her heart out.

"Shane's figured out who Benjie's father is and has threatened to tell him."

Tatum drew back. "Why would he do that?"

"Because…" It was more difficult for Cassidy to admit than she'd imagined. "Because he's Benjie's uncle."

Tatum slumped in her chair. When she spoke, there was no judgment or censure in her voice. "I assumed as much."

In all these years, Cassidy hadn't told a soul other than

her mother about Hoyt being Benjie's father. The fewer people who knew, the less chance of her secret getting out.

She'd suspected Tatum had guessed. How could she not? They were close, after all. But for right or wrong, Cassidy had chosen to remain mute.

Tatum had respected Cassidy's wishes and never pressed her to reveal the father's name, proving just what a good friend she was.

"What are you going to do?"

"I'm not sure yet." Cassidy shrugged. "For the moment, Shane has agreed not to tell Hoyt. But he won't be put off forever. He believes Hoyt has the right to know and wants me to tell him."

"Would it be all that terrible?"

Cassidy gaped at her friend. "What if he tries to take Benjie away?"

"He can't. There's no cause."

"I lied to him."

"Still not reason enough. You're a good mother."

"He can get visitation. And shared custody if he were to move here."

"Which he probably won't."

"I don't know for sure."

"All right. Let's say he does move to Arizona and gets shared custody of Benjie. What's the worst that could happen?"

Leave it to her friend to be practical.

"Benjie could decide he'd rather live with his father." Her voice shook.

"What's to say that wouldn't happen anyway? You've been lucky so far. Benjie hasn't shown much interest in his father. But chances are he will one day. Perhaps soon. Better you tell him while you're still able to control the circumstances. At least, to a degree."

Cassidy couldn't feel more out of control.

"Break the news to Hoyt," Tatum continued, "but wait until you're ready. Get your ducks in a row first. Talk to Deacon. If he can't help you, he'll recommend someone who can."

Cassidy saw the logic in her friend's suggestion. Her future brother-in-law was an attorney, and Cassidy would need one to advise her of her rights. Also inform her of Hoyt's rights and Benjie's, too. Then she could put together an informed plan of action.

"You're right." She sighed. "Thanks."

"It might not be all bad, you know. Telling Hoyt. There'll be child support. Someone who can help with other expenses, if not pay for them, like braces and college."

"I can find a way."

"No doubt. But why do everything on your own if you don't have to?" She stopped Cassidy before she could answer. "Right, right. To keep Benjie with you. Well, let's face it. Single motherhood isn't all it's cracked up to be. I, for one, am incredibly grateful for Ryder's help. He's great with the kids, and they love him. Hoyt's a nice guy. He could be just as great with Benjie."

"He drinks and drives. I don't want him putting Benjie in the same position he did me."

"That happened once, a lot of years ago."

"What if Hoyt hasn't changed?"

"Talk to him. Establish ground rules."

"Mom tried with Dad. He didn't listen."

Tatum studied Cassidy's face. "What's the real reason you haven't told Hoyt? Your father's alcoholism?"

"Please don't give me the speech about how he's sober now."

"I'm not talking about his drinking. I'm talking about the fact that, after six months, you two still can't seem to patch things up."

"One has nothing to do with the other." Cassidy sounded defensive, even to her own ears.

"You don't have a good relationship with your father. Can you honestly say he has no effect on your feelings about Benjie's potential relationship with Hoyt?"

"Hoyt's married. You don't think his wife will be upset he has a child with another woman?"

"I think you're making up excuses." Though Tatum's tone was gentle, her words were harsh. "Plenty of spouses deal with children from a previous relationship. Your brother, for instance. We're getting married, and I have three children."

"Hoyt's going to be furious with me."

"Or he'll be like Shane and your dad, overjoyed to learn he has a child."

After a moment, Cassidy admitted, "I'm afraid. Of a lot more than Benjie possibly leaving when he's older."

Tatum smiled. "Now we're getting somewhere."

"What if I tell Hoyt and it tears the family apart?"

"Your family? Why would it?"

"I've been lying. Like my mother."

"They overcame that." Tatum squeezed Cassidy's hand. "They will this, too."

As much as she appreciated her friend's support, Cassidy wasn't convinced. "I'm just not sure."

"What does Benjie want? Have you asked him?"

She shook her head and, sniffing, wiped at her nose.

"Cassidy, honey, don't you think it's time you did? After all, this is his father."

"He'll say yes. He wants to meet Hoyt."

"Maybe. Probably. But if you introduce them now, he'll be thrilled you did. If you deny him, he'll likely come to resent you."

Confusion muddled her thinking, and she rubbed her temples.

"There's Shane, too," Tatum mused. "And your relationship with him."

"That was a long time ago and nothing special."

"I'm talking about now." Tatum gave her a knowing look. "Anyone can see you two like each other."

"We do." There was no one she could admit her feelings for Shane to other than Tatum. "Which is why him pressuring me to talk to Hoyt feels a little like betrayal."

"Talk to Deacon," Tatum urged.

Cassidy nodded, feeling caught between a rock and a hard place. Whichever direction she took, she was going to collide with something sharp, and the resulting injury would be painful and possibly permanent.

THE JAMBOREE RODEO didn't technically begin for another four hours, though registration opened early in the morning. Trucks and trailers were arriving in a steady stream. Already the overflow parking area in the back pasture was half-full. Food and merchandise vendors were busy readying their wares for sale. Horses had been washed and brushed, tack cleaned and polished, clothes laundered and pressed.

At this moment, all Beckett hands were on deck. Each family member and employee had been assigned a specific job. Even Benjie was helping the maintenance crew ready the arena, though, truth be told, he was riding along on the tractor with Kenny while the teenager graded the deep dirt.

Cassidy kept watch on her son from the announcer's booth. She'd originally gone up there to run an equipment test. With everything in working order, she had no reason to remain, other than the booth also enabled her to observe Shane.

Just the sight of him caused her chest to tighten. She'd

stopped trying to decipher her emotions days ago. There were simply too many to separate.

He'd remained true. To her knowledge, he hadn't told Hoyt about Benjie. At least, she hadn't received a phone call from Hoyt, angry or otherwise.

Trusting people. It was a new experience for Cassidy. Other than her mother, sister and Tatum, there was no one else she relied on implicitly to put her best interests first. She certainly didn't trust her father or, to a lesser degree, her brother. Ryder had abandoned her when she was just twelve. Yes, they'd come a long way in recent months, but inside she was still a lost little girl, deserted by the ones she loved.

She ignored the chronic throb in her head, the one that had started last weekend during Benjie's birthday party and had plagued her all this week. Instead, she continued watching Shane, wondering what it might be like if they didn't have these issues between them. She might well be dating him again. Part of her wanted that. A large part.

At the moment, he was herding specialized livestock, acquired just for the rodeo, into temporary pens which had been set up near the practice ring. Sheep, to be specific, for use in the Mutton Bustin' competition. The miniaturized version of bull riding—children six and under got to ride a sheep—was a popular event at the Becketts' rodeos. The child who stayed seated the longest won first place, though every participant received a token prize.

Shane's daughter, Bria, followed him around like a second shadow. She seemed to exhibit both a fascination with and fear of the sheep, who were a noisy, active and smelly lot. Cassidy had overheard Shane earlier, trying to convince Bria to enter the Mutton Bustin' competition. From the vehement shake of the little girl's head, he hadn't succeeded.

The two of them were quite sweet together. Shane certainly had a way with her. He had a way with all children, apparently, as Benjie adored him. The baseball glove, bat and ball had strengthened the growing bond between the two of them. Most days, Shane and Benjie practiced pitching and hitting in the backyard before dinner.

Shane knew he was playing ball with his nephew. Knew now that his daughter's cousin was a mere fifty feet away, hitching a ride on the tractor in the arena. How, Cassidy wondered, did he feel? Was his chest as tight as hers?

Following Tatum's advice, she'd called Deacon. He'd given her the name of an attorney in east Mesa who practiced family law. During their phone call, the woman had put some of Cassidy's concerns to rest, but raised others. They'd scheduled an appointment for next week. Cassidy had wanted to meet sooner, as she wasn't sure how long she could put off Shane. Unfortunately, the attorney didn't have an opening.

Another week with her chest perpetually tight and this damn headache plaguing her 24/7. The stress had long since begun to show, increasing the number of times each day someone commented on her drawn expression and lack of focus.

She was about to leave the booth when she saw Shane kneel in the dirt in front of Bria. Had something happened? From this distance, Cassidy couldn't tell. Shane was clasping both of Bria's shoulders as if to comfort her, then kissed her forehead.

Last night during practice, Cassidy had watched him tangle with one of the horses. After dumping its rider, the horse had circled the arena at a full gallop. Shane finally cornered the horse and narrowly avoided being struck by a flailing hoof when it reared.

Cassidy had choked back a cry. Only when he had the horse under control had she released her death grip on the arena railing. She hadn't run over and hugged him like before, though the idea had crossed her mind. How could it not? The sensation of his arms around her invaded her thoughts continually.

No denying it. He was strong and capable and confident. All traits she admired…and happened to find attractive. They weren't half as attractive as the traits he displayed with his daughter. Gentleness, compassion, kindness. They drew her to him and made her think about him in ways she hadn't thought of a man in…she couldn't remember when.

He stood, a hand remaining on Bria's shoulder. Perhaps sensing Cassidy, his gaze lifted to the announcer's booth. A small shock wave reverberated through her, but she didn't look away. Smiling, he tugged on the brim of his cowboy hat. She returned the acknowledgment with a nod before leaving the booth, closing the door behind her and descending the narrow stairs.

An hour later, clipboard nestled in the crook of her arm, hand-held radio clipped to her belt, Cassidy navigated the growing crowd. Her mother and sister could probably use some assistance in the registration booth, and she considered going. The line snaked halfway to the office. Mostly, she was killing time until she was needed at the arena.

Benjie was with Tatum's three children, all of them under the care of the nanny Cassidy had hired for the weekend. The expense was a bit beyond her budget, despite Tatum chipping in for half, but she needed assurance her son was well supervised while she worked.

Her mother's and Tatum's words replayed in her head. Cassidy didn't disagree. Child support payments from Hoyt would definitely ease the tight pinch of her finances. The question was, would they be worth the cost?

An overwhelming need for a moment alone—this was becoming a habit—prompted her to change course. There was bound to be less activity behind the barn.

There was also Shane's trailer. How could she forget?

He opened the door and emerged, spotting her before she could get away.

"Hey." He grinned, not a single trace of the tension she'd been battling all week evident in his carefree expression.

Her mind promptly shut down at the sight of him. He looked good. Better than good. Dressed in a clean Western-cut shirt, fitted jeans, black leather vest and matching black Stetson, he could have easily graced the pages of the hot cowboy calendars her sister used to keep before meeting Deacon.

"Whatcha up to?" He stepped down onto the ground and made straight for her, no hesitation in his stride.

"I was, um…" The excuse she'd been prepared to give died on her lips as his proximity breached her defenses. "Frankly, I needed a break."

"I understand. It's been rough lately."

She closed her eyes, bone weary. "That's an understatement."

"Want to come in for a cup of coffee or a cold drink?" He gestured at the trailer's still open door. "I could use a pick-me-up."

"Where's Bria?"

"With DeAnna and her family. Your mom was generous enough to give them free passes. The sleepover's set for tomorrow."

"I'm guessing her mom checked out."

"A real nice lady. I took your advice and paid her a visit the other day. I'm sure Bria will be fine. If not, I'm ten minutes away."

"I'm glad."

"I was serious about having coffee."

Cassidy knew she should decline. Until she decided what to do about Hoyt, it was best she maintain strict boundaries with Shane. But she didn't decline. As one of the four people who were aware of her situation, she could be herself with him. There was something liberating about that.

"Okay."

He moved aside and she entered the trailer ahead of him. The steps creaked as she ascended them. Creaked louder when Shane did. Was it a warning? Had she made a mistake by accepting his invitation?

Shane crowded behind her. Even if she wanted to escape, it was too late now. She was committed to seeing this harebrained idea through to the end.

Chapter Seven

The trailer was more cramped than that first day, Shane has settled in, but Bria's things were also everywhere. A doll on the table. Her overnight bag in the corner by the closet. Sneakers on the rug in front of the kitchen sink.

Signs of Shane abounded, as well. He obviously wasn't the best housekeeper. Neither was he the worst. A canvas laundry bag hung from the bathroom door knob, a shirt sleeve poking out. A towel lay crumpled on the floor beneath the laundry bag. Through the doorway to the sleeping area, Cassidy saw the haphazardly made bed.

He must have read her thoughts for he apologized. "Excuse the mess. No time to clean up today."

Cassidy found herself smiling. "I have a six-year-old boy. I've seen much worse than this. Trust me."

"I do. Trust you."

He studied her intently, and a familiar, warm sensation bloomed in her middle. She didn't resist it.

"Funny," she said. "I was thinking the same thing myself. That maybe I could trust *you*."

"Maybe?" Humor tinged his tone.

"It isn't easy. I've been hurt in the past."

"By Hoyt?"

She shook her head. "Not hurt so much as other things."

"Such as?" Shane removed his vest and cowboy hat,

hung both on a peg, then selected two coffee mugs dangling from hooks beneath the cupboard. Filling them with water from the tap, he added instant coffee and heated the mugs in the tiny microwave.

"He disappointed me," she said. "Angered me. But, in hindsight, I think the relationship was already circling the drain. I was probably looking for an excuse to end things."

"What happened?"

"Hoyt never told you?"

"I'm interested in your version."

"He liked to party a lot. It was after the Down Home Days Rodeo. He'd won three events and was celebrating with his buddies. I wanted to go back to the hotel room and told him I'd catch a ride with a friend. He insisted on driving me, but I knew he'd been drinking. I wouldn't go with him and accused him of not caring."

"That wasn't like him."

"I agree. But like I said, we were all but broken up." She shrugged. "He knew I was raised by an alcoholic father and had a low tolerance for any kind of dangerous behavior. He could have been testing me. Or picking a fight."

"I'm sorry, Cassidy." Shane moved Bria's doll from the table and set down the coffee mugs. He reached into the narrow pantry. "You take creamer and sugar?"

"If you have it." She sat, laying her clipboard and radio on the seat beside her.

Shane slid in across from her, his manner unhurried. Apparently, he was going to let her tell the rest of the story at her pace.

"I didn't know I was pregnant when we broke up."

"Why didn't you tell him when you found out?"

She stirred creamer and sugar into her coffee. "I thought if he cared so little for me that he'd willingly put me in danger, how would he be with our child? I realize now I was scared. My life was completely turned upside down. I had no clue what I was going to do. I didn't want to marry Hoyt and worried he might insist on it. I wanted less to come home, single and pregnant. My mother had sacrificed everything for me, and I was at the peak of my rodeo career. A shoo-in for state champion. I'd have to give that up in order to raise my baby. Something I knew nothing about."

"Things seemed to have worked out for the best."

"They have. Benjie's a happy, well-adjusted kid."

"Then why haven't you told Hoyt?"

She sipped at her mug, letting the warm coffee soothe her frazzled nerves.

"I almost did." Strange, but telling Shane her story wasn't nearly as difficult as she'd anticipated. In fact, it was surprisingly easy. "I went to Topeka to see him when I was eight months pregnant. I changed my mind at the last minute, and came immediately home."

"Why?"

"I learned he was engaged. Another barrel racer told me." She met Shane's gaze across the table. "I didn't want to be responsible for ruining his marriage."

"What makes you think you would have?"

"Seriously?" She almost laughed. "You think Cheryl would have been okay with a pregnant ex-girlfriend showing up on their doorstep? And besides, she'd already lost a husband. I couldn't be the cause of her losing a second. She didn't deserve that."

"Hoyt's Benjie's father," Shane said. "He has a responsibility. He also has a right."

Cassidy could sense the conversation going in a direction she didn't want. "Doesn't change the fact it would have been an unexpected blow. One impossible to rebound from."

"If Cheryl called off the wedding because Hoyt fathered

a child before he met her, then maybe she wasn't the wife for him."

"I disagree. That's a lot to deal with, literally two weeks before your wedding."

"Okay. Let's agree to disagree. For the moment," he added without anger or rancor. "That still doesn't explain why you haven't told Hoyt since then."

She took a deep breath, then admitted, "Lack of nerve."

"Because of your brother and your fear Benjie will leave like he did?"

"That's not the only reason."

Shane waited, again giving her the chance to explain in her own time.

"I didn't want to be responsible for breaking up a second marriage," she confessed.

"Second?" He looked at her with interest. "You have another old boyfriend?"

"No." Cassidy hesitated. Twenty-five years later, and it still pained her to think about it. "My parents' marriage."

"The way I heard it, your dad's drinking caused their divorce."

"It did."

"I don't understand. How are you responsible for his drinking?"

"I'm not. I'm responsible for my mother not sticking by him and not giving him the chance to get sober."

"I'm still confused. You were just a kid."

She drained her coffee, hoping the caffeine would bolster her courage and enable her to finish revealing this very difficult part of her past.

"One night, my dad picked me up from a friend's house. He'd come straight from the bar and had no business driving. Mom would never have let him if she'd known about it. I didn't want to go with him, but neither did I want to make a scene in front of my friend. On the way home, he misjudged the distance, or wasn't paying attention, and plowed the truck into the well house."

"Were you hurt?"

"No, neither of us was. But it scared the hell out of me and afterward I had a meltdown."

"It's understandable."

"I demanded my mom send him away. Threw fits when she tried to reason with me. A couple weeks later, she did just that. Dad packed his bags and moved to Kingman."

"You didn't break up their marriage. It was already on the rocks."

"What if I hadn't insisted?" Difficult as it was for her, Cassidy met Shane's gaze head-on. "Everything, and I mean *everything*, would be different. Liberty would have known our father her entire life and not grown up confused and hurt, believing herself unlovable. Ryder wouldn't have left, breaking my mom's heart. My parents might still be married and not spent years being apart and miserable."

"Or your mom would have divorced him anyway."

"Ryder begged her not to. It was as if she chose which one of her children she loved more. I don't think he forgave me until recently."

"Cassidy, don't take this wrong, because it's a sad story and I can see you and your family are still coping with the fallout, but what does it have to do with Hoyt and you?"

She bit back a sob, refusing to let Shane see her cry. "I couldn't take the chance of causing him and Cheryl the same kind of misery I did my parents. Neither could I have lived with the guilt. I already have enough of that."

The confession left her oddly empty. And relieved. At the touch of Shane's hand covering hers, she looked down. His fingers, though calloused, were warm and comforting. She didn't resist. A moment later, she turned her hand over to clasp his.

It should have been surreal, her sitting here holding

Shane's hand. Instead, it felt natural. As if they'd been holding hands all their lives.

In retrospect, her rushing to his side and his kissing her cheek when Wasabi went on a rampage had also been natural. She hadn't stopped to think, and she didn't now. She just savored the moment.

"Your mother made her choice," he said. "She sent your father away because she wanted him gone."

"I think she was on the fence, and I pushed her over onto the side of divorce. They love each other to this day. He came back to Reckless for Liberty, but also to marry Mom again, which makes me feel guiltier."

"Is that what she wants, too?"

"Not at first. He's made a lot of progress lately convincing her otherwise."

"You're not to blame, Cassidy. She and your dad were adults. He could have chosen to get help with his addiction sooner than he did. She could have arranged an intervention. Gotten him into rehab. Leaving was hardly his only option."

"But what if I hadn't insisted she send Dad away? *Everything* might have turned out differently."

"Or your dad wouldn't have gotten sober when he did, and the next time he crashed the truck he might've wound up in the hospital."

She withdrew her hand from his. "That's a pessimistic outlook."

"I don't like to play the what-if game. I did it a lot after finding out about Bria and drove myself crazy with anger and regrets. None of us can change the past. The best we can do is move forward."

His cavalier attitude rankled Cassidy, but the more she considered his words, the more she saw the logic behind them.

"I have been driving myself crazy."

"You don't know what Hoyt and Cheryl would have done. Called off the wedding, postponed it, gone through with it. Just like you don't know what they'll do now when you tell them about Benjie. But after six years of solid marriage, I can't see her walking out on him."

She noticed he used the word *when*, not *if.*

"They're trying for a child," she said. "Cheryl could resent me and Benjie because Hoyt and I accomplished what the two of them haven't."

"Haven't yet. They've just recently started seeing a specialist."

"What if she takes out her resentment on Benjie?"

"You're doing it again. Playing what-if."

Cassidy's shoulders sagged. "I can't help myself."

"First off, Cheryl's not a resentful person. She's as nice as they come. Secondly, Hoyt isn't the same person you knew six years ago. He's grown up a lot. We both have."

She definitely agreed with the second part. Shane was nothing like the wild young man she'd gone out with. Never in million years would she have imagined herself revealing her deepest, darkest secret to him.

"I'm seeing an attorney next week," she abruptly blurted. "About custody of Benjie."

"Good."

"You're not mad?"

"Why would I be? It's a smart move on your part. Your first priority is Benjie."

He probably felt that way because of Bria. "I'll call Hoyt. After I've figured things out with the attorney."

Shane nodded. "Fair enough."

"You'll still wait? Not say anything to him until I do?"

"Of course. I could also be with you when you make the call." He took her hand again and squeezed. "If you want. For moral support."

Cassidy opened her mouth to say no, though that wasn't what came out. "All right."

She half expected him to gloat. Flash her an I-was-right-all-along smile. Instead, he caressed the back of her hand with his thumb, sending tiny arrows of heat along the length of her arm. Heavens, she was susceptible to him.

"What you're doing takes a lot of courage. If Hoyt doesn't realize that, I'll make sure he does."

"Thanks." She checked the clock on the microwave. "I'd better get going. Mom and Liberty are probably wondering where I am."

"Me, too. Don't want your dad to fire me for being late before my first rodeo."

They stood simultaneously. Shane grabbed his vest and hat and waited for her to enter the cramped space between the table and the door.

Hand on the knob, she hesitated.

"Something wrong?" he asked from behind her.

"I just want to thank you."

"Anytime. We're friends, Cassidy."

Friends. An interesting description, considering the sparks flaring between them since his first day at the arena and their brief, but romantic, past. She pivoted— and confronted the broad expanse of Shane's chest mere inches from her.

"Oops."

She should have moved. Turned back around and hurried outside. She didn't. It was as if finding him so close rendered her immobile. He didn't appear in a hurry to move, either.

Seconds ticked by. She struggled to slow her rapid breathing.

Lord have mercy, he smelled incredible. Masculine but not overpowering. She remembered thinking the same thing that first day in the trailer.

What might it be like to rise on her tiptoes and press her lips to his? She had half a mind to find out. Fortunately, she resisted the impulse.

"See you later," she said, and reached again for the door.

She didn't get far. Shane's arm snaked around her waist, stopping her. The next instant, he pulled her snug against him and lowered his head. Her eyes widened and her mouth opened in shock. He was going to kiss her!

I can't let him was her first thought. *I can't* not *let him* was her second. Suddenly she didn't want to go the rest of her life regretting this missed opportunity.

CASSIDY BECKETT. IN HIS EMBRACE. And she wasn't resisting. Shane almost didn't believe it.

He increased his hold on her, assuring himself this was completely real and not his imagination. Were he honest with himself, he'd admit to thinking of exactly this for weeks. He was human, after all, and a man, and he intended to take every advantage of this unexpected windfall.

He lowered his head and, burying his face in her neck, inhaled deeply. "You smell great."

She laughed nervously.

"That's funny?" He nuzzled the sensitive spot beneath her ear.

"Kind of. I happen to think the same thing about you." She angled her head to give him greater access to her silky skin. "That you smell great."

Did she now? He licked the same spot he'd been nuzzling, then sucked gently. Clinging to him, she gave a soft shudder. Shane was immediately hooked, on her and her incredible responsiveness.

He inhaled again, then withdrew to look at her, convinced he would never smell anything as wonderful again in his life, hold anyone as desirable. "You don't know how hard I've had to work at resisting you."

The laughter left her eyes. "I beg to differ," she said somberly. "I do know."

He had truly never wanted a woman more than he did in that moment. Didn't think he'd ever want another woman again after Cassidy. It wasn't just his lust talking, either. She appealed to him on every level, emotionally, spiritually and physically.

How had he not realized this before? Granted, they'd dated a short time and never gone much beyond kissing, but still…

Without pausing to ponder the importance of these new feelings for her, he dipped his head and captured her mouth with his. She gasped in surprise. He groaned, low. The combination of lips and tongues and hands roaming bodies was electric. And it only got better.

Cassidy arched against him, sending a spear of desire slicing though him. She was soft where a woman should be soft, firm everywhere else. Temptation in its purest form.

Good thing they'd waited before. At nineteen, he wouldn't have been ready for this. For her.

Convinced he might lose control, he fought to hold back. It proved impossible. Just as it would be impossible to ever forget her.

He couldn't get enough. Pressing his palm into the small of her back, he waited, not certain he could stop there. At the touch of her fingers sliding into the hair at the base of his neck, his thinly held control threatened to snap.

Deepening the kiss, he explored every delicious corner of her mouth. She might be letting him take the lead, but that didn't mean she wasn't a willing participant with an arsenal of moves designed to drive a man over the edge.

And it was working. Perfectly. Shane lost all track

of time and place. Hell, he could barely remember his name. There was nothing and no one but Cassidy and him, wrapped together in this small trailer at the very center of the universe.

If not for the chug-chug of the tractor driving practically beneath the trailer's window, they might have gone on kissing indefinitely. Cassidy stiffened and pulled away.

"Sorry." He wasn't, but he felt obliged to apologize. "I got a little carried away."

"You weren't acting alone."

Thank goodness. "It was some kiss." Kisses, as in many, each and every one seared in Shane's memory.

She brushed a lock of disheveled hair from her face, the gesture self-conscious, yet incredibly sexy. When she lifted her face, she wore a tentative smile.

His relief didn't last long.

"I don't regret kissing you," she said. "That doesn't mean I think it should happen again."

"I disagree."

"Shane, getting involved isn't a good idea. Not now. Not until this situation with Benjie and your brother is resolved."

"I don't see what difference it makes."

She shook her head. "Things are complicated enough."

He inhaled and took an emotional step back. "I agree. They are. But we're entitled to be happy."

"Hoyt may not like me getting involved with you. I can't have him adding challenges to our custody negotiations because he resents my relationship with his brother."

"He isn't a shallow person."

"This is brand-new territory. None of us knows how the others will react. I can't take the chance."

She had a point. "Okay."

"Really?" She studied him skeptically.

Shane was smart enough to realize if he pushed Cassidy she'd dig in her heels and he'd lose all the ground he'd gained. Best to agree with her for the moment then, when the dust settled with Hoyt, make his next move. He could wait. She was worth it.

Reaching behind her for the knob, he opened the door. "Really. Now let's both get back to work before the boss catches us goofing off."

She laughed and exited the trailer, Shane right behind her. Once outside, she paused. He did, too, and she placed a hand on the center of his chest.

"For the record, I enjoyed the kiss."

Did she feel his thundering heart? "Me, too."

"It was never like that before."

"Not even close."

Lifting her hand to his face, she cupped his cheek, her fingers lingering before she turned and left.

Shane stood, watching, until Kenny emerged from the outdoor stalls, leading a pair of arena horses used for steer wrestling. He nodded at Shane, a silly grin on his face.

Had he seen Shane and Cassidy together? Shane wasn't sure—the teenager often wore a silly grin for no reason. He promptly put Kenny from his mind. What had there been to see, other than her cupping his cheek? Nothing inappropriate there.

At the arena, he got straight to work, though his and Cassidy's recent kiss wreaked havoc with his concentration. Bull riding was traditionally the last event of the day, being one of the most exciting and crowd pleasing. That didn't give Shane leeway to sit around, doing nothing. The care and condition of the bulls was his main concern. Especially Wasabi, who had been cleared to compete. However, this decision made no difference to Shane. He intended to check over every inch of the bull before letting him in the arena.

In addition to the eighteen bucking bulls the Becketts

owned, they'd leased an additional twenty for the weekend from their competitor, the Lost Dutchman Rodeo Company. Shane had spent the entire day yesterday involved in transporting the bulls from nearby Apache Junction.

It was Mercer Beckett's ambition to purchase more bulls over the next several years. A high-earning bull could bring in tens of thousands of dollars a year, if not into the hundreds of thousands. There were several potential contenders in the Becketts' current stock.

The future also looked bright for another reason. Just prior to hiring Shane, Mercer had purchased a number of champion-producing cows. Breeding would begin shortly and become the next phase of Shane's new job.

"Is Wasabi ready?"

Shane glanced over his shoulder at the sound of Mercer's voice and stepped away from the larger of the two bull pens. "In my opinion, yes."

"We're counting on him."

Something in his boss's tone gave Shane pause. Was this a simple question or his make-it-or-break-it moment? Did his future at the Easy Money depend on Wasabi's performance? If so, he was ready for it.

He squared his shoulders. "I don't think you have anything to worry about."

"I hope so." Mercer took a place at the fence alongside Shane, resting his forearms on the top railing. Inside the pen, the bulls milled restlessly, lowing and swinging their large heads from side to side. They instinctively sensed this was no normal day. In every direction, people bustled about. Cowboys readying to compete. Fans eager for a close-up of the rodeo stock and exhibitors. The Verde Vaqueros equestrian drill team practicing for the opening ceremony.

"Kenny noticed Cassidy coming out of your trailer earlier," Mercer said, his tone flat. "He said the two of you were pretty cozy."

Not what Shane had been expecting, and he steadied himself before answering.

"We're old friends."

"Not just friends. She dated your brother. My grandson is your nephew."

Startled, Shane turned his head. Had Cassidy kept her secret only from Hoyt and the Westcotts? "How long have you known?"

"Always. Leastwise, I suspected. Most people did, I reckon."

Not Shane and Hoyt. Were they idiots? Maybe not. If one wasn't looking, he supposed, then one didn't see.

"I don't want Cassidy hurt. Or Benjie," Mercer said.

"I care about both of them. And Benjie's family."

"Take it from me, family can hurt a person worse than any stranger."

"I won't lie. I did ask her on a date."

Mercer muttered a response under his breath. "What about your brother?"

"Doesn't matter. She declined. For the time being," Shane clarified. "She wants to speak to Hoyt first."

"And after that?"

"We'll see what happens."

"Look, son. I'm not judging." Mercer adjusted his hat, shielding his eyes from the bright midday sun. "Lord knows, I have my own complicated family situation. But you need to tread carefully. My grandson has taken quite a shine to you. Cassidy, too. I can see it. If not, she wouldn't be hesitating, waiting to talk to Hoyt first. She's cautious when it comes to men. I reckon I'm the one to blame."

Shane didn't like to think of Cassidy struggling. He did like to think her fondness for him was strong enough to be evident to others.

"I won't hurt her."

"You can't promise that."

"I assure you, my intentions are honorable."

"What about your daughter?"

"What about her?"

"You haven't had custody long. She might resent you dating Cassidy."

"She adores Benjie. I think she'd be thrilled to learn she has a cousin."

"You could be right." Mercer pushed off from the fence. Clapping a hand to Shane's shoulder, he squeezed. "I'm glad our family is increasing in size. And that your daughter's a part of it. You, too, as long as Cassidy's happy." The pressure of his grip increased, almost to the point of painful. He stopped just short. "If for any reason things change, you'll have me to deal with. And there'll be a lot more at stake than your job."

Shane didn't flinch. Didn't blink an eye. "Understood, sir."

"Do you mind telling me what's going on here?" Cassidy stood facing them, her laser stare taking aim at Mercer.

Shane gave the older man credit, who reacted by letting his hand drop and shrugging unconcernedly. "Just having a talk. Man to man."

"You're butting into a matter that doesn't concern you."

Shane had been prepared to stay out of the argument. Cassidy wasn't one to trifle with when riled. Neither was Mercer. They were more alike than they probably realized. He changed his mind when he noticed the attention the three of them were garnering.

"The opening ceremony starts in an hour," he said. "Maybe we should move along."

"Good idea." Mercer approached Cassidy. Rather than walk past her, he stopped and bent his head, kissing her on the cheek. She stiffened but, otherwise, didn't move. "We'll talk later, sweetheart."

"Count on it."

Shane thought it best he, too, leave. He'd have liked to kiss Cassidy, as well. Common sense prevailed.

"I'm sorry about that," she said, catching up with him.

Well, this was a day full of surprises. "Your dad loves you."

"It's too little, too late."

"Only if you let it be."

"There's still a lot you don't know."

Shane stopped abruptly. "This is a conversation you need to have with him. Not me."

She stiffened. A moment later, she was gone, disappearing into the crowd.

Mercer didn't have any reason to worry about Cassidy getting hurt, Shane thought with disappointment. Judging by her brusque departure he doubted they were going on a date, now or in the foreseeable future.

Chapter Eight

"Thanks for everything. I'll be in touch." Cassidy tucked the representation agreement she'd signed into her purse and shook the woman lawyer's hand.

"I can't recommend contacting the father strongly enough. If he finds out about Benjie before you've told him, he could, and likely will, use that against you. He already has a lot of ammunition, what with you holding out this long."

"I'll call. This week."

"Today, if possible," the attorney insisted. "His brother may have promised to remain silent, but there's no guarantee he will."

"I trust him."

"Don't. In my experience, there are two times when loyalties are tested and family members choose sides. When someone dies and when there's a custody battle over the children."

Cassidy could think of another time. When one member was an alcoholic.

"That's rather dismal."

"But unfortunately true." The attorney offered a warm and supportive smile. Her first one of their entire meeting.

Cassidy braced a hand on the corner of the desk to steady herself. Was she ready to talk to Hoyt? No, but then, would she ever be? Getting it over with quickly might be the best approach. Then, hopefully, she could go back to sleeping soundly at night.

On the drive home from Globe, she mentally reviewed her meeting with the attorney. She'd liked the middle-aged woman's assertive manner and had hired her on the spot. The advice she'd offered, and her no-punches-pulled honesty, hard as it had been to hear, resonated with Cassidy. She'd be a strong advocate for Cassidy and Benjie when it came to dealing with Hoyt's attorney, as he was sure to hire one.

Shane had offered to be with her when she called Hoyt. The attorney had visibly recoiled when Cassidy had told her and insisted he be excluded. At first, Cassidy had agreed. Now she was having second thoughts. Shane was fiercely loyal to his brother, but he also cared for her, of that she was certain, and wanted what was best for her.

She recalled their steamy kiss from last Friday—something she'd done often during the past five days. It was one of those mistakes a person would make all over again given the opportunity. If she concentrated, she could feel the tingles cascading up and down her spine. The warmth pooling in her middle. The desire weakening her limbs.

Tingles and warmth aside, she wasn't planning on any more kissing. Not before she and Hoyt reached an agreement. Possibly not after that. The situation was too tricky, and she had her son to think of.

Shane also cared a great deal about Benjie. If he wasn't present when she spoke to Hoyt, she'd for sure have him there when she told Benjie. Her son already felt a strong bond with Shane. If Benjie wound up reacting negatively, Shane would be a good person to calm him and ease his fears.

Unless Hoyt objected. What if he didn't like his brother

interfering with his nephew? She hadn't considered that before.

Because her mind was spinning a hundred miles an hour, she opted to delay deciding until later. Upon entering Reckless, she spontaneously turned into the Dawn to Dusk Coffee Shop for a caramel latte. Her favorite. After a day like this one, she deserved to indulge herself in some comfort food. Or a comfort beverage, as it happened to be.

She was next in line to be served when someone came up behind her and cut in.

"Excuse me," said an irritated customer. "I was here first."

Cassidy whirled to find Shane standing there, cheeks ruddy from the wind and smelling of the outdoors.

He moved closer and tipped his hat to the woman customer. "Sorry, she was saving me a place."

Caught off guard, Cassidy had no choice but to allow him in line with her. She gave the woman customer her nicest smile and was rewarded with an agitated huff.

They reached the counter and placed their orders. "I'll buy," Shane said and removed his wallet from his jeans. "Hers, too." He indicated the woman behind him.

"Oh, thank you!" she said.

Cassidy wasn't so easily mollified. She still hadn't forgiven him for cutting in line. "Fine," she told the cashier, "I'll have a tall."

"Where were you today?" Shane asked as they waited for their coffees. "You left and didn't tell anyone."

"I wasn't aware I had to report in with you."

Not the first time she'd been short with him this week, and it was wrong of her. Truthfully, she was mad at herself and taking it out on him. Hardly Shane's fault that she'd practically ravished him in the trailer, then argued with her father in front of him.

"You don't, but we were worried."

"I told Deacon."

"He wasn't anyone we thought of asking."

Shane's repeated use of the word "we" puzzled her. Was he including himself with her family?

"I went to see an attorney in Globe. I didn't want to tell anyone until I saw how it went."

"And?"

Shane didn't have a right to ask her. This was none of his business. And the attorney had soundly advised her against including him. On the other hand, she'd included him earlier by discussing Benjie and her plans for telling Hoyt. She supposed he felt he had the right.

"It went okay."

The barista called their names. Shane retrieved the steaming cups.

"Let's sit outside." He all but hustled her to the shop's exterior seating area.

She went along. She didn't want to talk in the noisy and crowded shop. It seemed more people than usual were free for coffee at one o'clock on a Thursday afternoon. Shane being one of them.

"Wait," she said. "You didn't tell me what you're doing here."

"I was headed to the feed store for some supplements. I saw your SUV parked out front."

Just her luck, or bad luck depending on one's point of view.

They found an empty table for two under the awning. It wasn't warm. In fact, the temperature had dropped this week to the upper fifties. But it was bright out, and Cassidy's tired eyes were grateful for the awning's shade.

"So, what did the attorney say?"

She chose her words carefully, not intending to reveal everything to Shane in case the attorney was right about choosing sides.

"She told me what I can realistically expect to happen. What I can reasonably ask for from Hoyt. And what the worst case scenarios are. We also discussed strategies and options."

"I think you just said a lot of nothing."

Cassidy sipped her coffee, relishing the taste and warmth. "I'm not going to discuss details with you. Not until I speak to Hoyt."

"Is that what the attorney suggested?"

"It's what I want. What I'm comfortable with."

"How much of you shutting me out has to do with our kiss the other day?"

She tightened her grip on her cup. "We agreed not getting personally involved was for the best."

"We did. But when did not getting personally involved include stop being friends?"

"Hoyt's your brother. Your loyalties are understandably with him."

"Believe it or not, the person I'm most loyal to is Benjie."

Damn. He *would* have to say the right thing.

"For various reasons, the attorney recommended that I call Hoyt as soon as possible. Today, specifically."

Shane rubbed his chin, considering her remark. After a moment, he said, "There's no time like the present."

"I'm not calling him now." Cassidy glanced around nervously, which was silly. None of the nearby patrons were the least bit interested in them.

"It's as good a time as any. I'm here. You're here. I know for a fact Hoyt's off this week."

She shook her head vehemently. "The attorney was clear. She said I shouldn't call Hoyt with you present."

"I won't sabotage you."

She believed him, mostly because of the remark he'd made about Benjie. She didn't want to call Hoyt alone.

With an audience, she'd be more inclined to keep a level head. Not lose her temper or her courage.

"I need some paper," she blurted. "For notes." And for something to do with her hands that didn't involve biting her nails to the quick.

Shane pulled a small notepad from the pocket of his jacket. On the top sheet was a list for the feed store in small, blocky printing. Why she would notice now, she had no idea.

"Here." He set the pad in front of her, then reached inside his jacket. The next instant a ballpoint pen lay atop the notepad.

He had everything at the tips of his fingers. *How convenient*, she silently groused.

Pulling her phone from her purse, she stared at it, her nerves deserting her at an astounding rate. Eyes closed, she willed them back.

"I'll dial for you."

"What?" Her eyes snapped open.

"Hoyt's number. I'll dial it for you."

She passed him the phone, grateful he wouldn't see the tremors in her fingers making dialing impossible.

God, it was here. The day she'd been dreading and avoiding for over six years. She resisted the urge to flee to her SUV and drive far, far away. That wouldn't solve anything. But, oh, how she wished differently.

"Here." Shane handed her the phone.

The device felt heavy in her palm. She almost couldn't lift it to her ear. At the sound of ringing on the line, everything and everyone faded into the background, and she was left alone, standing on the edge of a steep cliff.

More ringing. Maybe she'd catch a break and Hoyt wouldn't answer. Then what? Should she hang up and call back later? Leave a message? God, what would she say?

The choice was taken from her when the call connected, and life as she knew it, the world she'd carefully constructed for herself and Benjie, entirely and irrevocably changed.

"Hello. This is Hoyt Westcott."

Cassidy couldn't speak. Her mouth, it seemed, had gone completely dry. Her lips refused to work properly. Her mind had emptied all coherent thought.

"Ah…ah…"

She couldn't do it. Regardless of what her attorney said, she'd wait until next week when she was more prepared. Next month. Next—

Shane whipped the phone away from her. "Hoyt," he said, "it's me." There was a pause. "Yeah, well, I'm calling you from Cassidy's phone." The next pause seemed to go on forever. At the same time, it was over much too soon. "She has something to tell you."

And, again, the incredibly heavy device was placed in her hands and pressed to her ear. How could that have happened without her remembering?

"H-Hoyt. How are you?"

"I'm good. How 'bout yourself?"

He sounded the same, if a little hesitant. Then again, what had she expected? Passing years and being married would change his voice?

A small glimmer of hope sparked inside her. He'd always been easygoing and jovial. If he was still the same, then maybe he'd be reasonable and cooperative about Benjie. Not mad as hell and determined to get back at her for lying.

Cassidy went numb all over. Please, she silently prayed, don't make this hard.

Aloud, she said, "Um, I'm all right. Is this a good time to talk?" Maybe he would say no.

"It's great. We just got back from taking Cheryl to the doctor. She's resting now."

"Is she all right?"

"Fine. A routine exam. We're hoping for a big family," he added haltingly.

"Oh. Yes." How could she have forgotten?

What if Cheryl didn't conceive and the fertility treatments failed? How would that affect custody of Benjie? Because of the distance, Cassidy's attorney had recommended allowing Hoyt to visit frequently. But, for the time being, he only take Benjie to Jackson Hole twice a year: four weeks over the summer and either Thanksgiving or Christmas.

Cassidy considered that doable, though the idea of Benjie being away for nearly half the summer left her with an empty ache in her heart. She simply couldn't live with him being gone any longer.

"I don't want to disturb you," she told Hoyt. "I'll call back next week."

Across the table, Shane gave her a look. "It won't be any better next week," he said in a low voice. "And it might be worse."

At first, she was angry. Who was he to tell her what to do? Then she realized the remark was meant to be encouraging. And, much as she hated to admit it, he was right. There was no going back now. She must tell Hoyt. Better to get it over with.

"This is as good a time as any," Hoyt insisted, closely echoing Shane's earlier comment. "What's up?"

"There's something I need to tell you. Haven't told you," she amended, still stalling.

He waited. And waited. "Cassidy?"

"When we broke up... I was..." *Breathe. Breathe. It's going to be okay.* "I was pregnant."

"You were?" He sounded startled. And confused. "Why didn't you tell me?"

"I didn't know it. Not for a few weeks."

His voice grew increasingly strained. "What happened? To the baby?"

"I had a son. His name is Benjamin. Benjie, for short."

"A son." Dead silence followed.

Cassidy spoke in a rush to fill it. "He's six. Just had a birthday. That's how Shane figured it out."

Hoyt went from sounding startled and confused to accusatory. "Is that why you're telling me now? Because Shane got wise?"

Technically, she was telling him because her attorney had recommended it. Better not to mention legal representation just yet. That could create a problem where there wasn't any.

"I was planning on telling you. Shane's discovery did speed things up."

"Planning on it? The kid is six years old."

Here came the anger Cassidy had been anticipating and fearing.

She glanced at Shane. Like that day in the trailer, right before they kissed, he reached across the table and took her free hand in his. His kind smile said she could do this. He was with her every step of the way, and she could depend on him.

Returning her attention to the phone, she continued, "What matters is I'm telling you now."

"Sorry," Hoyt said. "I don't buy that. You don't do anything without a reason."

"All right. I'm telling you because I'm backed into a corner." More silence. Was she wrong to have been completely honest? "Hoyt?"

"This is a lot to assimilate," he finally said. "I need a minute."

"Take your time."

"Why not tell me before?" he repeated, with less animosity this time.

She supplied him with a boiled-down version.

"I was scared. Of a lot of things. Mostly, I thought you'd pressure me into marrying you, and I wasn't ready for that. Later, I changed my mind. I flew to Topeka to tell you and learned you and Cheryl were getting married. It didn't seem like the right time to spring the news on you that I was eight months pregnant."

"I'd have taken care of you and our son."

Our son. She always referred to Benjie as *her* son.

A very large, very painful lump formed in Cassidy's throat. Dammit. She didn't want to get emotional. If she wasn't careful, she'd fall apart, and she desperately needed to remain in control. Hoyt's next words, however, snapped her tenuous hold in two.

"I want to see him. Soon."

The attorney's advice resounded in Cassidy's head, warning her not to refuse any reasonable requests. Pick your battles, she'd said. Compromise on the small stuff. Stand strong only on the big stuff.

"All right. We can arrange a visit. Benjie has Monday off school next week—"

"Tomorrow."

Air rushed out of her lungs. "No. Impossible!"

"You've kept him from me for six years. I won't wait, Cassidy."

The threat was subtle but there. Would a judge say, because she'd hidden Benjie from him for six years, Hoyt could have him for the next six?

She refused to let him steamroll her. Back when they were dating, Hoyt had believed he could win every argument simply with a show of force. That, along with his immaturity, had caused their relationship to deteriorate.

"Next weekend," she insisted. "You can come out Friday morning and spend the long weekend in Reckless. That'll give me time to tell him about you and that you're coming for a visit. Also give you time to tell Cheryl about him."

"He doesn't know about me?"

"No."

"What *did* you tell him?"

His earlier anger had returned. She had to proceed cautiously. "His father was a cowboy I had dated and cared about greatly, but things didn't work out."

"A father who didn't want him?"

"It's not like that, Hoyt." She tried to keep the strain from her voice. Shane squeezing her fingers helped calm her and keep her focused. "I told him when he was ready, he could meet you."

She didn't add that, thus far, Benjie hadn't shown interest in meeting his father. Hurting Hoyt's feelings wouldn't gain her anything. Besides, it was unkind.

"What does he like? To play with, I mean." The change in Hoyt's tone was abrupt. "I want to bring him something."

"Well, recently, he's gotten into baseball." She looked at Shane, who responded with a nod.

"A glove?" Hoyt suggested.

"He has one already."

"A bat, then."

Why hadn't she suggested something else? "Lately, he's been building model cars and planes. The simpler ones."

"I did, too, when I was his age."

She could hear the smile in Hoyt's voice. It tore at her heart much more than she would have expected and gave her pause.

Hoyt wasn't the enemy. She'd been wrong to label him that way for all these years. He'd been young and made a stupid mistake, insisting she come with him when he'd been drinking. That wasn't reason enough to hide his son from him. Nor was the possibility of ruining his upcoming marriage. It was an excuse Cassidy had latched onto rather than face the real reason.

No maybe about it. Her mother had hit the nail on the head when she'd said Cassidy's refusal to tell Hoyt was connected to her unresolved issues with her father.

Did everything have to keep going back to her parents and their divorce? How could one event impact so many people and completely change the course of their lives? Cassidy was tired of coping with the aftereffects.

Collecting herself, she said, "Why don't you call me back when you've worked out the details of your trip? Then we can make plans." And Cassidy could arrange another appointment with her attorney. Just to get more of those concerns laid to rest.

"Can you email me some pictures of him?"

Cassidy blinked, taken aback, though she shouldn't have been. "Of course."

"Shane has my email address."

She might have said goodbye, she couldn't be sure. The last seconds of the phone call had become a blur. Tears filled her eyes and she laid the phone down on the table.

"You did good." Shane hadn't moved. He continued to sit across from her, his hand squeezing hers.

Cassidy had occasionally imagined telling Hoyt about Benjie. In none of those versions was Shane there, comforting and consoling her. She liked reality better. He was making this difficult day a tiny bit more bearable.

"If you want, I can help you tell Benjie."

She wiped at her cheeks. Already, her tears were drying. "I do."

Possibly, she was making a huge mistake by allowing Shane to get closer. Then again, he might be the one person she needed most to survive the weeks ahead.

Chapter Nine

Benjie wriggled and tugged at the collar of the shirt Cassidy was attempting to button up.

"Please, sweetie," she coaxed. "Settle down."

"I don't like the shirt."

"But you picked it out." Wanting him to look his best for this first meeting with Hoyt, she'd driven him into Globe yesterday specifically to buy him a new outfit. Benjie had chosen a pair of Wranglers—go figure—and a Western-cut shirt that looked a lot like the ones his uncle Shane wore. Cassidy didn't think it was a coincidence.

"This is itchy," he complained and tugged again on the collar.

She doubted that. More likely, her son was nervous. They both were. Cassidy had been in a constant state of agitation since her conversation with Hoyt—which intensified a few days ago when he called to advise her of his travel plans.

Telling Benjie that his father and his father's wife were coming to meet him had gone surprisingly well. Since his birthday, and especially since meeting Shane and Bria, Benjie had been fixated on the idea of a father. All of a sudden he had one, and he couldn't be more excited.

All week he'd pestered Cassidy with questions. What was his father's name? Where did he live? What was he like? Was he a champion bull rider like Uncle Shane? Did he look like Uncle Shane? Did he play baseball like Uncle Shane?

Sometimes, Cassidy thought he was more excited about Shane being his uncle than Hoyt being his father.

Then, yesterday, the questions began to change, as did Benjie's mood. He became untypically reserved and quiet.

"What if he doesn't like me?" he asked her again.

Cassidy bent and fed his belt through the loops on his jeans. "He likes you already and can't wait to meet you."

"Do I have to go see him in Wyoming?"

She had tried to explain the possible visitation schedule and now regretted it. "Jackson Hole is nice. Very different from Arizona."

"But what if I hate it there? I won't know anybody."

"Nothing's been decided yet." She gave Benjie a hug before straightening.

"What do I call my stepmom?"

She'd also tried to explain the whole stepfamily concept. It was a lot for a six-year-old to comprehend.

"She and your father will tell you when they get here."

Cheryl. Cassidy had been pondering her a lot lately. Was she friendly and personable? Patient and even tempered? Would she resent Benjie because of her own difficulty conceiving? Worse, what if he liked her? Would Cassidy be jealous?

Benjie crossed his arms and stuck out his lower lip. "I don't want him to take me away like Grandpa took Uncle Ryder away."

"Oh, sweetie." She smoothed his hair, then kissed the top of his head. She should have been more careful and not let him overhear her conversations with her family. "Grandpa didn't take Uncle Ryder away. It wasn't like that."

"But Uncle Ryder left."

"Because he wanted to."

"Well, I don't want to leave." The lip extended farther.

"Then you don't have to."

They finished dressing soon after that, and Cassidy told Benjie he could watch TV while they waited. She'd purposely gotten him ready early in order to give herself plenty of time to shower and change before Hoyt and Cheryl's arrival.

She was just buttoning up her own shirt when a soft knock sounded on her bedroom door.

"It's me," came her mother's voice from the other side.

"Come on in."

"How are you holding up?"

"Not bad, I guess."

"Tell me the truth." Her mother perched on the edge of Cassidy's bed. "You're white as snow."

"Am I?" She caught a glimpse of herself in the dresser mirror. Good grief, she was pale. "It's been a tough week."

"I'm proud of you, honey. What you're doing takes courage."

People, including Shane, kept telling her that. Cassidy didn't feel courageous. She felt scared out of her wits.

"I can't lose him, Mom."

"You won't."

"But what about Ryder? He left." The assurances she'd given Benjie were all for show. Deep down, she dreaded the possibility.

"It's not the same. Benjie doesn't resent you."

"He might. When he's older, he could figure out I prevented him from seeing his father for the first six years of his life and resent the heck out of me. Hoyt could poison his thinking. Cheryl could be the wonderful, fun stepmother who overindulges him while I'm the mom who makes him do his homework and clean his room."

"You're letting yourself get carried away. For all you know, Benjie and Hoyt won't get along."

"That's not what I want."

"Of course you don't. My point is, we can't foresee the future. The best we can do is take each day as it comes."

Cassidy plunked down on the bed beside her mother, who put a comforting arm around her shoulders.

"We're here for you if you need us."

We, Cassidy surmised, meant her mother *and* father. "You and dad are getting pretty cozy lately."

Her mother gave Cassidy a squeeze before releasing her. "I won't deny it."

"You didn't come home last night."

"I'm a grown woman." There was a cheerfulness in her mother's voice Cassidy had been hearing more often lately.

"If you're happy, then I'm happy."

"I am. More than I thought possible."

"What if he regresses? Alcoholism doesn't go away."

"I doubt he'll regress. He hasn't touched a drop for over twenty years."

"You've made quite a turnaround. When Dad first returned to Reckless, you fought him tooth and nail at every step."

"Things are different. You children are grown, for one."

"Yeah, but you have a young grandson living here. Let's just say, for the sake of argument, that Dad—"

Her mother cut her off. "Take every day as it comes, remember?"

It was a bad habit of hers, anticipating the worst. Also a difficult one to break.

A glance at the bedside clock made Cassidy jump to her feet, heart racing. "They'll be here soon."

Her mother also stood, though considerably more

slowly. "I'd really like for you and your dad to patch things up. He wants it, too."

Cassidy pushed her hair off her face, breathing deeply in an effort to relax. "Can we talk about this later? Please. I have enough to worry about right now."

"I understand." At the door, her mother paused. "Just give it some consideration, okay? It would mean a lot to both of us. Your brother and sister, too."

"Sure."

Why, for heaven's sake, was her mother pushing a reconciliation now, of all days? Had something changed? Cassidy was too rushed to give the matter more than a passing consideration. Benjie's voice carried from the other end of the house, followed by thundering footsteps.

"Uncle Shane!"

He'd slipped so easily into calling Shane "uncle." She should be pleased. Shane certainly was. His booming voice also carried down the hall.

"How are you, buddy? Ready for the big day?"

Walking toward the kitchen, Cassidy could imagine Shane lifting her son into his arms as he often did. She stopped just before the entryway and silently observed them.

They were exactly as she'd pictured them in her mind, both grinning broadly. Cassidy marveled at the slight resemblance she hadn't noticed before. It was more mannerisms than anything physical. "Is my dad like you?" Benjie was clearly still bursting with questions.

"In some ways. He's also different than me."

"How?"

"He's taller. I'm a better bull rider."

"Is that true?"

"Would I lie?"

Benjie giggled, and Shane lowered him to the floor, ruffling the hair Cassidy had meticulously smoothed not thirty minutes ago. "Actually, you're a lot like him. Funny. Smart. Gregarious."

"What's gregorus?"

"Outgoing. Enough energy for two kids."

"Mom's always telling me to calm down and go slow."

Shane glanced at Cassidy and gave her a wink. "She was always saying that to your dad, too."

Had she? Cassidy couldn't recall. Then again, she had surprisingly few memories about her relationship with Hoyt. Had she purposely tried to forget? Pushing him from her mind with the same diligence she'd pushed him from their lives?

She berated herself for being selfish. Regardless of how her relationship with Hoyt had ended, she should have preserved their memories for the day when their child would ask. Certainly the good ones, and there had been some happy times.

"I wish you were my dad." Benjie's proclamation caused both Cassidy and Shane to stare at him, Cassidy with her mouth open.

"Sweetie, no." She had no idea how to respond. "Don't say that."

"But it's true." He pouted, all trace of her charming little boy gone.

Shane went down on one knee in front of Benjie. "Hey, look at me, buddy."

Benjie did. Reluctantly.

"It's scary. Meeting your dad for the first time. I know because Bria had to go through the same thing when she met me. But I'll tell you a secret."

"What?"

"This is just as scary for your dad."

Benjie shrugged.

"I don't know what kind of dad he'll be, but I can tell you he was a pretty great big brother. Stuck up for me when I got in trouble or was picked on. Helped me with my homework. Played with me. Took care of me. He'll do the same for you. All you have to do is give him a chance. Okay?"

"Okay."

Shane stood and pulled Benjie to his side. "That's my boy."

Tears gathered in Cassidy's eyes, undoubtedly the first of many today. Clearing her throat, she edged closer.

"Hoyt and Cheryl should be here any minute."

"They're probably pulling in the driveway now," Shane said. "Hoyt called a few minutes ago."

"So soon!" Alarm filled Cassidy—and might have overtaken her if not for Shane's steadying hand on her arm.

"Relax. Everything's going to be all right."

She believed him—for exactly three seconds. Then, the front doorbell rang.

SHANE SAT IN the far corner of the living room couch, watching the goings-on and keeping his mouth shut. The situation was hard enough on everyone without him making comments.

But, if he was to speak, he'd tell his brother to dial it down a notch. Overwhelming the poor kid with a big personality and a bright, shiny gift wasn't going to win him over. He should just take it easy and be himself. Then, maybe, Benjie would stop clinging to his mother and squeezing into the slim space between her and the arm of the wingback chair where she sat.

Shane would also tell Sunny that being the perfect hostess wasn't necessary. Once the tray of lemonade was delivered and the glasses filled, she should have skedaddled out of there. An audience wasn't helping. Shane would be gone, too, if Hoyt hadn't insisted he stay and Cassidy didn't look as though she was ready to splinter into a dozen pieces.

Of all of them, he felt the worst for Cheryl. This was what she wanted. A child. The longing in her eyes was heartbreaking. She attempted to cover it with a forced smile, sickeningly pleasant small talk and a chin-up attitude.

Maybe she, Sunny and Shane should leave. Let Benjie and his parents figure things out on their own. How to suggest that? He was interrupted by Benjie's first real contribution to the conversation.

"Uncle Shane plays baseball with me every day."

Hoyt looked over, his expression difficult to read. "He does?"

"More like catch," Shane clarified.

"And we go horseback riding," Benjie said.

"Only a couple times."

"Shane's been very good to Benjie." Cassidy placed her hand on Benjie's head. The gesture could be interpreted as motherly...or protective. "They've become close."

Whatever was going on, Shane didn't want to be a part of it. Regardless of his feelings for Cassidy, he had no intention of usurping Hoyt's place in Benjie's life. "I've been telling him a lot about you and stories from when we were kids."

"Do you like to fish?" Hoyt asked Benjie.

"Never been."

The gift he'd brought was a new youth-size rod and reel. A good idea, considering Roosevelt Lake was a mere thirty minutes away and the fishing there some of the best in the state.

"Maybe you should go while you're here," Shane suggested. "Your dad's a pretty good angler."

"What's that?" Benjie asked.

"A fisherman."

Benjie peered at Hoyt with new interest, then twisted in the chair to look at Cassidy. "Can I, Mom?"

"We can certainly talk about it."

The tension in the room, already high, increased.

"Cookies anyone?" Sunny rose. "I have homemade chocolate chip."

Shane considered chasing after Sunny and waylaying her in the kitchen, just to give the rest of them some privacy. Unfortunately, she was too fast for him, so he did the next best thing.

"Hey, Benjie. Why don't you take your dad to the barn and show him Skittles?" When Cassidy nearly exploded from her chair, he added, "Your mom, too. We'll have cookies when you get back."

"Okay." Benjie was suddenly all smiles. "You come, too."

"I'm going to wait here. Keep Cheryl and your grandmother company."

His sister-in-law looked almost relieved. Not Benjie, who fixed a stubborn scowl on his face.

Shane was trying to think of what to say next when his brother surprised him.

"Skittles, huh? I've ridden that horse. Years ago. I was competing in the Wild West Days Rodeo. Calf roping. My horse threw a shoe. Your grandmother let me borrow Skittles." Hoyt smiled and exchanged glances with Cassidy. "I came in second place. You remember?"

"I do. You beat out Shane."

Her voice had softened, and a tiny smile touched her lips. Shane was completely enamored and, for just a second, forgot where they were and why.

Benjie giggled, his interest in his father at last genuine. "You beat Uncle Shane?"

"He barely qualified, as I recall."

In calf roping. But Shane had taken home the gold

buckle for bull riding. "Your dad was always a better roper than me."

"I can't believe Skittles is still around." Hoyt slapped his thigh. "I'd like to see him. If you'll take me."

"We have to hurry." Benjie jumped up and grabbed Cassidy's hand, pulling her out of the chair and across the room to where Hoyt sat. "Grandpa feeds at five o'clock. We're not allowed in the barn then."

Hoyt stood and patted his son on the back. "We'd best get after it, then."

Benjie forgot all about including Shane, for which he was glad. He wouldn't trade his relationship with Bria for anything in the world and wished the same for his brother.

At the entryway from the living room to the kitchen, Cassidy paused and glanced over her shoulder. He nodded encouragingly, trying to let her know she was doing just fine, and he'd be right here when she returned.

"Thanks for helping," Cheryl said to him after the others had left. "This has been a strange and strained day."

"Where did everyone go?" Sunny appeared holding the tray of cookies and wearing a perplexed expression.

"They needed some time alone." Shane snatched a cookie off the tray and took a bite. "Good," he muttered.

"Hmm." Sunny set the tray on the table and motioned to a chair. "Would you two like to join me?"

"Thank you." With a what-else-can-I-do attitude, Cheryl sat.

She was making the best of a difficult situation, a quality Shane admired. He liked his sister-in-law and had always thought her a good match for Hoyt. More serious than her husband, she grounded him without dragging him down or smothering his outgoing nature.

Cassidy was also serious, but with a razor-sharp intensity that, when ignited with just the right match, turned into a fiery passion. Shane liked igniting that passion. When the time was right, he'd do it again.

"I'll take a rain check," he told Sunny and grabbed another cookie on his way out the door. "The bull riding jackpot starts at six."

Two weekends every month, when there wasn't a rodeo, the Easy Money hosted bucking stock events. For a reasonable fee, participants entered a nonsanctioned competition. A portion of the entry fees were set aside, with the top three scores for the evening splitting the pot. The popular event had increased in recent months with the addition of new, championship-quality bulls like Wasabi.

Shane assumed his brother would come looking for him when he finished with Cassidy and Benjie. He wasn't worried when he stopped at the trailer for a quick bite of supper before the jackpot. He wasn't worried an hour later when the jackpot got underway. An hour after that, he was having trouble concentrating. Every few minutes, his gaze wandered toward the barn or the house.

Where were they? How was it going? Had something happened? Should he call Hoyt?

Shane was ready to dispatch one of the hands to look for them when he spotted Cassidy sitting alone in the last row of the bleachers.

"Kenny," he hollered to the teenager. "Cover for me. I'll be right back."

Spectators' heads turned as he bounded up the bleacher steps two at a time. Cassidy's wasn't one of them. She was so lost in thought, she didn't glance up until the vibration of his boots hitting the floorboard roused her. Even then, she didn't appear to recognize him for several seconds. When she did, she turned her head.

Catching his breath, he lowered himself onto the seat next to her. "How'd it go?"

Her answer was to cover her eyes with her hands. It was then Shane realized she'd been crying.

"Hey. Don't do that."

Without thinking, he nestled her in the crook of his arm. At first, she tensed. The next moment, she slumped and leaned her head against his shoulder. Shane didn't disturb her, even when his arm fell asleep.

Chapter Ten

Cassidy suppressed a groan. How had this happened? Once again, she'd let Shane breach her defenses. Why was he the one who evoked feelings in her she'd rather keep buried? The one who knew without being told what she needed? Today, it was unconditional support without questions.

"I'm not a crier," she said at last, lifting her head from his shoulder and wiping her damp cheeks with a tissue procured from her jacket pocket.

"You cry. You just don't let people see you."

How true. Figures he'd see right through her pretenses. "Sorry." She straightened, putting a few inches between them. His arm slipped from around her shoulders.

Much better, she thought. The distance, slight as it was, lessened her vulnerability to him.

"Did Hoyt and Cheryl leave?"

"A while ago. Mom's watching Benjie for me."

Cassidy had attempted to calm her son after his father left—*his father* still sounded so strange to her—without much success. Benjie was over the moon. Once the ice had been broken and common ground discovered, thanks mostly to Skittles, he and Hoyt had talked nonstop. Cassidy had barely gotten a word in until the end of the visit. For all she knew, Benjie was still talking.

When her mother had offered to forego the bull riding jackpot and take over Benjie's nighttime routine, Cassidy had jumped at the chance, desperately needing to get away and recover emotionally and mentally from a trying afternoon.

Out of habit, she'd wandered to the arena. Any other evening, she, too, would have been working the bull riding jackpot. No one had been sitting in the uppermost row of the bleachers until Shane had joined her. Before she could tell him to go, he had sat down. At the time, accepting the comfort he'd offered seemed natural. Lord knows she could use a friend.

Now she was less sure. What if he jumped to the wrong conclusion? She was already having a hard enough time keeping him at arm's length. Sitting with her head on his shoulder, for twenty minutes according to the clock on the electronic scoreboard, sent the wrong message.

"Am I wrong to assume things didn't go well?" he asked. "I wondered when Hoyt didn't find me to say goodbye."

"Things went great."

"They did?"

She summarized Benjie and Hoyt's successful visit.

"Is that what has you upset? The visit going well?"

"I am so shallow." She sniffed and rubbed her nose.

"You're scared. Which is perfectly normal."

"I don't want to lose Benjie." Her chest hurt as if every bit of air was being squeezed from her lungs. "I can't."

"Hoyt won't do that to you."

Cassidy wanted to believe him, but there were too many variables. "You know what upsets me the most?" She couldn't believe she was about to confide in Shane.

"What?"

"Seeing Benjie with Hoyt. It was…sweet. And kind of endearing."

He chuckled. "That's not so terrible."

"Maybe." She'd had the same reaction when she saw her son and Shane together. Then, she hadn't felt as threatened.

"Did Hoyt mention visitation?"

"We didn't go into details. That's for the attorneys to hash out. But he swears he'll be reasonable. He also asked me to bring Benjie to Payson next month while he's there working."

"Okay. That's not asking too much."

She sighed. "No, it's not."

"I could go with you. Bring Bria. Before Hoyt learned about Benjie, we agreed I would drive up and meet him for the day."

They could hardly sit next to each other without touching. A two-hour road trip would stretch their willpower to its limit. Then again...

"I'll think about it. Thanks for the offer," she added. They watched the bull riding for several minutes in silence. Then, Cassidy surprised herself by saying, "I would like you to come with us tomorrow."

"What's happening?"

"Hoyt suggested a trail ride with a picnic lunch. I'm not comfortable letting him and Cheryl take Benjie alone. When I expressed my concern, he said that, naturally, I could come along."

Which had irked her. As if *Hoyt* got to invite *her* along on an outing with *her* son.

"Maybe you should stick to the four of you."

"I already told him I was inviting Ryder, Tatum and her three kids." Safety in numbers, as far as she was concerned. "I think Benjie will be more comfortable that way."

"Okay," Shane mused aloud. "If Hoyt doesn't mind."

She wanted to say the hell with how Hoyt felt. Instead, she simply nodded. "We're leaving at eleven."

"I'll need to be back by three. Doc Worthington is stopping by."

"We all need to be back by then." Saturdays were always busy at the Easy Money.

Another several minutes of silence passed, after which Shane said, "Hard as it is, you're doing the right thing."

"Yeah." Her voice cracked.

"You're not going to cry again, are you?" His tone was teasing. The look in his green eyes was mesmerizing.

She couldn't bring herself to look away. "No, I'm not."

He touched her cheek, wiping away a tear with the pad of his thumb. "Too late."

Damn it. She hated him seeing her like this.

Before she could stop him, he brushed his lips across hers. The kiss was tender and comforting. Night and day from the smoldering one they'd shared in his trailer. Yet desire pulled at her, stronger than ever.

How could he do that with the merest of touches? She blamed the fact she hadn't been kissed by another man in a long, long time. Also, she'd been an emotional wreck this past week.

The truth was, she wanted Shane. With a desire that terrified her as much as it thrilled.

"You should know," he said, his voice low and husky and raw with need. "I'm going to kiss you."

Hadn't he just done that?

"If you don't want me to, you'd better get up and leave right now."

She should have thanked him for the warning and run for the hills as fast as her legs could carry her. Instead, she remained seated, willing him to make good on his promise.

"There's no going back after this, Cassidy."

Back to what? Her lonely life?

This had been one of the hardest days she could ever remember. She wanted Shane to take her to heaven and make her forget, if only for a minute. Or, two. Maybe three.

"What are you waiting for?" She tilted her head and parted her lips. "Kiss me."

Shane didn't hesitate and covered her mouth with his.

She let him take control, abandoning all resistance. It was wonderful. Freeing, actually.

Her hand sought his jaw and stroked it. The stubble from his five o'clock shadow tickled her fingertips. She liked the sensation so much, she went in search of others, finding the silky texture of the fine hairs at the base of his neck and the strong muscles of his neck and shoulders.

A groan emanating from deep inside his chest distracted her. He withdrew long enough to whisper against her lips. "You are incredible."

Was she? Shane made her feel that way. Incredible and sexy and desirable. It was a heady combination, and an addictive one.

"Tell me to stop," he said.

"And if I don't? Will you kiss me again?"

His answer was to make her every romantic dream come true. She clutched the fabric of his vest in her fists, pulling him close and sealing their lips together. He, in turn, wrapped his arms around her. Never had they been closer. Had more intimate contact. Been more attuned to each other.

Too far!

The words exploded inside her head and caused her to abruptly pull back. "Wait."

"What's wrong?"

"Slower." She expelled a long breath. "I need to go slower."

"I can kiss you as slow as you want." One corner of his mouth quirked in his trademark disarming grin.

"No more." She placed a restraining hand on him. "Not tonight." And not in front of all these people.

"All right. As long as it's not for good. It's not for good, is it, Cassidy?"

"I need some time." She had to stop letting him kiss her. Stop kissing him back.

"You're right. I'm sorry. I took advantage of you." He eased away.

"No more than I took of you," she admitted.

He smiled. "Feel free to do that anytime the mood strikes you."

"Shane." Her pleading eyes searched his.

"I get it." Patting her leg, he stood. "I'll see you tomorrow. At the trail ride."

"Tomorrow," she repeated.

The next instant, he was gone.

She should be thinking about Benjie and Hoyt, the trail ride and the changes coming at her like a freight train traveling full steam ahead. Instead, she missed the warmth of Shane's body. The scent of his skin. The taste of his lips.

It was scary how quickly she'd gotten used to him. Scarier how miserable she'd be if he left.

THE WEATHER HELD. Cassidy had worried up until the moment they set out on the trail ride that they might be rained out. Slowly, the clouds transformed from dark and gloomy to a washed-out gray. Other than the periodic gust of wind, it wasn't a bad day. Weather-wise or otherwise.

Hoyt and Cheryl hadn't expected it, but along with Ryder and Tatum's children, *all* the Becketts accompanied them, including Cassidy's parents, and her siblings and their respective future spouses. When ascending the first hill in single file, the line of horses they rode stretched better than thirty yards from first head to last tail.

Liberty brought up the rear, leading a coal-black mare she was training for a client. The young horse carried a pack saddle. Inside was the light picnic lunch Sunny and Cassidy had quickly assembled. Cheese spread, crackers, beef jerky, individual cups of applesauce and leftover chocolate chip cookies comprised their fare.

Ryder rode double with Tatum's youngest son seated in front of him. Other than that, everyone had their own mount. Shane, Cassidy couldn't help observing, stayed close to her. Perhaps because Benjie stayed close to Hoyt. Either way, she appreciated his presence.

Her hands ached from constantly gripping the reins too tightly, and she forced her fingers to relax. A moment later, they strained again. *Stop it*, she told herself. All was going well. Nothing bad had happened. There was no reason for her angst. Yet there it was. By the end of their first hour she was exhausted.

When they reached a long flat area on the south ridge and her father announced this was probably as good a place as any to break for lunch, she was more than ready. Hopefully, stretching her legs for a bit would relax her. Calm her. Distract her.

While the four children darted to and fro, burning off excess energy, the men tethered the horses to any available low-slung branch. Sunny and Cheryl distributed the food. Cassidy should have helped. Her mind, however, refused to settle down, and she wandered aimlessly.

Finding a large rock to use as a stool, she sat, took a long pull from the bottled water she'd brought in her saddlebag and watched the children play. Benjie, younger than Tatum's oldest by a year, was still taller. He had inherited his height from Hoyt, as well as his outgoing personality and his sense of humor, which, in Benjie's case, often manifested itself in class clown behavior.

What had he inherited from her other than his looks? Cassidy didn't think of herself as timid. More like guarded. And cautious. She wasn't one to leap without first looking. Funny, at Benjie's age, she'd been just as adventurous. Just as carefree. Her father's drinking had changed her. After the accident and her parents' divorce, she'd become a whole different person.

Speak of the devil…

Her father approached. "You doing okay?"

"Fine," she automatically replied. No one ever wanted to hear the truth.

"Mind if I join you?" He lowered himself onto the rock beside her.

"Not at all." Did she mind? Cassidy wasn't sure.

That in itself was interesting and new. She'd spent the last six months being angry at her father and making every effort *not* to be alone with him. Now, all of a sudden, she didn't care?

"You okay?" he asked. "You seem preoccupied."

"It's been a rough week. A strange week."

"I can relate."

He probably could, no doubt to Hoyt.

For the first time, Cassidy was curious about her father's reunion with her younger sister. "What was it like, meeting Liberty after all those years?"

"Weird." He gave a low chuckle.

"Seriously."

"I am serious. Took me weeks, months really, to get used to the idea. Not that I didn't love her right away. But she was a stranger to me, and me to her. I wanted us to instantly click. Instead, it took time."

"Benjie and Hoyt are clicking."

He followed her gaze to where Hoyt and his wife sat

with Benjie, eating their lunch. "It does look that way on the surface."

Cassidy wasn't sure what to make of his remark. "You think they aren't?"

"Hoyt's trying hard. Too hard. Though I understand his motives. But he needs to rein it in a bit. I did the same with your sister. Rushed the connection before either of us was ready, and it backfired."

"Benjie's excited to have a father."

"Sure he is. But watch him closely. The initial thrill is wearing off, and even if he doesn't realize it, he's starting to wonder what impact this new dad is going to have on his life and if all the changes will be good ones."

She hadn't realized her father was so perceptive, or so deep. He was noting the same subtle differences in Benjie she'd observed these last two days.

The man apparently had sides to him she'd yet to see. Sides, she admitted, were intriguing to her.

"What makes you say that?"

"He asked me before the ride if Hoyt planned on taking him to Wyoming."

Cassidy sighed heavily. "My fault. He's heard me telling the story of when Ryder left. I should talk to him again."

"You and Hoyt should *both* talk to him. Assure him he has nothing to fear."

Why hadn't she thought of that? She was the worst mother in the world, concerned only with herself.

"I will. We will," she amended. "After the ride."

Several moments passed in silence. The three older children, having finished their meals, were pleading with Shane to join in their antics. Why not Hoyt?

Perhaps because Shane wasn't trying too hard the way Hoyt was, at least, according to her father. Shane was also someone the children knew better. Visiting only periodically, Hoyt might never be someone Benjie knew well.

She turned to her father. "Would you have come back more often if you'd known Liberty was your daughter?"

"Absolutely. Regardless of the grief your mom gave me." He removed a pack of gum from his shirt pocket. She accepted when he offered her a piece. "Not sure I'd have moved back permanently, but visited, yes. Frequently."

"Was it hard on you, being so far away from me?" Cassidy hadn't realized how desperately she wanted to learn the answer to that question until she'd asked it.

"It was terrible. I missed you something awful," he said earnestly. "I'd have visited more often if you hadn't hated me like you did. Still do, at times."

"I was angry," she defended herself. "With good reason. And I didn't...don't hate you."

"Sometimes it's hard to tell the difference between the two. Anger and hate."

Guilt consumed her. If she hadn't treated her father in such a cold manner, her parents might still be married and Ryder wouldn't have left. "I'm responsible for the rift in our family."

"Not at all, baby girl." He brushed a knuckle along her cheek. "That's my fault entirely. I'm the one who drank away the arena's profits. The one who drove while intoxicated, with you in the passenger seat, and ran the truck into the well house. I'm the one who let your mother down time and again and divided our family."

Baby girl? He'd called her that endearment when she was little.

Memories from years ago promptly assaulted Cassidy. Unlike before, these weren't painful or hurtful. They were lovely and sentimental.

She could see the two of them walking across the back pasture, her small hand enclosed in his larger one. Four, maybe five years old, she'd begged him to take her to pick the wild hollyhocks, their large, delicate white blossoms in stark contrast to their coarse stalks. Another time, he'd found her in the haystacks, sobbing after the family dog died unexpectedly from an infection, and comforted her with a story of dog heaven.

It hadn't always been bad between them. Mostly it had been good. Ryder had tried to tell her, but she wouldn't listen. Shame on her.

"If I could do it over again," her father said, "I would. Fight harder for you. Truthfully, I'm not sure what I regret more. Losing out on knowing your sister for the first twenty-four years of her life or the night of the accident."

The moment had come for Cassidy to atone. Six months ago when her father returned—heck, last month before Shane showed up—she wouldn't have said that. How things had changed. And how incredibly quickly.

"I'm the reason Mom divorced you."

He chuckled again. "I hardly think so."

"No, it's true. After the accident, I was scared. I insisted she make you leave. I forced her to choose, and she picked Ryder and me over you."

Her father sat back and scratched his whiskered jaw, a bemused expression on his face. "Your mother isn't that easily manipulated. Believe you me, she wanted me gone."

"Because I insisted."

"Because of my drinking and its effect on our lives."

"I ruined your marriage."

"While I'd like nothing better than to lay the blame at someone else's doorstep, if there's one thing I've learned in twenty-plus years of AA meetings it's no one's responsible for my marriage hitting the skids other than me. I had choices, and I made one wrong one after the other."

Cassidy looked for Hoyt. He'd taken Shane's place with

the children. Benjie beamed up at him, obviously hanging on his every word.

Had she made a mistake not telling Hoyt the truth all those years ago?

Her father, mother and Shane, they were each of them right. She couldn't alter the past. The best she could do was affect the future.

"Thanks, Dad." She squeezed his hand, feeling the walls between them slowly crumble. It was a shame they hadn't had this talk before, though Cassidy wouldn't have been receptive.

He beamed at her with the same joy her son showed Hoyt. "You have no idea how long I've waited to hear you say that."

"Say what?" She smiled.

"*Dad*, with just that tone."

She glanced away, afraid her face would reveal the depth of her emotions. "I can be stubborn. And difficult."

"You're your mother's child." He tucked his finger beneath her chin and lifted her face to his. "Makes me love you all the more."

Impulsively, she threw her arms around his neck and hugged him close. Not the same as saying she loved him in return. Still too many walls between them. But it was close. And enough for now. The rest, she was suddenly confident, would come.

"Well, well, well," he said, his voice gruff. "That's the nicest thing to happen to me in quite a while."

She released him slowly and said softly, "Same here."

Neither of them moved from the rock. Rather, they enjoyed their newfound closeness in mutually agreeable silence. It lasted until Benjie came running up to Cassidy.

"Can I have another cookie?"

"Sure." Why not? she thought. Nothing said celebration like a chocolate chip cookie, and she had reason to celebrate today.

Benjie scrambled back to Hoyt, carrying not one but two cookies.

"He'll do right by Benjie," her father said, referring to Hoyt.

"You think? I've kept my distance from him for six years. I have no idea what kind of person he's become."

"Give him a chance."

"I will." Before, she'd felt cornered. Pressure coming at her from all sides. Today, the pressure had been lifted. "Shane's a great dad. I never saw that coming. He was every bit as wild as Hoyt back in the day."

"Shane's been through a lot. Nothing like staring your future in the face to mature a person."

"Are you talking about his fall from Wasabi last year?"

"No, his daughter."

Cassidy was staring her future in the face, too, and it wasn't easy.

"I know you got mad at me the other day for interfering in your relationship with him."

"You were out of line," she agreed.

"Only because I care about you."

She now knew that to be the real reason, whereas she hadn't before.

"I approve of him for you. He's got backbone and strength of character, which he'll need plenty of."

Cassidy narrowed her gaze at her father. "Because I'm stubborn and difficult."

"Because you stand up for your convictions," he said, with a fondness in his voice that made her smile. "And if Shane isn't bursting with admiration for you like I am, he's not the man for you."

She shook her head. "I'm not ready for a relationship."

"No one ever thinks they are. That's what makes it wonderful when it happens."

"You're talking about you and Mom."

"Mark my word, I'm going to marry her."

He'd been saying as much all along. But until today, Cassidy hadn't supported the match. Funny how one's perspective could be suddenly altered.

"Mom's a long ways from being convinced."

"She'll get there." He winked at her, then pushed to his feet. "I'd better check on the kids' horses. Benjie's saddle looked a little loose during the ride. Girth probably needs adjusting."

After giving her shoulder an affectionate pat, he left, stopping first to talk to Cassidy's mother. She could see the love and devotion in his face. What would it be like to have a man look at her like that? She searched out Shane, finding him engrossed in conversation with her brother. Probably about arena business.

She supposed she should get after it, too. Help with the cleanup and run herd on the children. The last person she expected to come over and give her a hand was Cheryl.

"Here, let me," she said and bent to collect the empty juice boxes strewn on the ground.

"Thanks." Cassidy held open the trash bag.

"It's absolutely beautiful up here."

"I've always loved this spot."

What an incredible day, Cassidy mused. Benjie playing with Hoyt. She and her father having their long overdue reconciliation. Working together with Cheryl and casually conversing.

"Hey." Shane appeared beside her, his green eyes alight with curiosity. "Your day must be improving."

"Very much so."

"I'm intrigued."

She took in his rugged, handsome features and the easy

grin that always started her heart fluttering, and smiled in return. No reason the day couldn't continue to improve. All she need do was open herself to the possibilities.

Chapter Eleven

By the time they returned from the trail ride, the arena was in full swing. Tom Pratt had scheduled his popular calf roping clinic. This was the renowned expert's third such event at the Easy Money and, with each one, attendance increased.

"Hey, sis." Ryder sidled up to Cassidy, his voice dripping honey. "You mind taking care of our horses? Deacon and I are heading over to watch Tom."

"No problem. Have fun."

"You sure?"

"Get out of here."

"Our horses" turned out to be Ryder's, Deacon's, Tatum's and the two her children had been riding. Cassidy shrugged off the inconvenience, glad to have something to keep her busy.

"I owe you," Tatum said when she discovered that Cassidy had been burdened with the job.

"It's okay." She smiled at her friend, who would have helped but was taking care of her youngest. The toddler had complained of an upset stomach during the ride home. "You can do me a favor sometime."

"Count on it."

Benjie wasn't so lucky. Rather than getting off the hook, he had to unsaddle, brush and put away Skittles.

The task went from being a chore to something fun when Hoyt stepped in to help. Cheryl had mentioned during the cleanup that she and Hoyt were having dinner in Mesa with a local rodeo promoter and his wife. They would return in the morning to spend the day with Benjie and again on Monday for a last visit before flying home.

One at a time, Cassidy led the horses down the barn aisle to the hitching post outside the tack room where she unhurriedly tended them. When she was done, she returned them to their stalls and went back for the next horse.

She was just finishing with the last horse when Hoyt strolled down the barn aisle.

"Mind some company?" he asked when he neared.

"Not at all." She peered behind him. "Where's Benjie?"

"With Cheryl and your mother."

"Oh." That was unexpected. Hoyt hadn't ventured three feet from Benjie all day. "How is Cheryl handling all this?" For some, the question might be none of their business. Cassidy felt she had a right to know.

"She's doing okay," Hoyt said.

"It must be hard on her, you having a child when you've both been trying for quite a while without success."

"She's glad for me."

Cassidy didn't doubt it. But neither was Cheryl made of stone. She must be hurting to some degree. Would it get worse during the summer when Benjie visited?

"Tell her she can call me anytime. If she has questions about Benjie."

"She doesn't need parenting advice from you, Cassidy."

Her defenses rose. "Benjie's my son."

"Mine, too."

So much for things going well. Cassidy had enough of this mild sparring. Hoyt's next words let her know they weren't done, not by a long shot.

"Cheryl and I have been talking. I want to be an active father."

"Of course." A spark of nervous energy traveled through Cassidy. Was he leading up to a demand for additional visitation? Custody?

"Not just when I visit, either," Hoyt said. "I'd like to be included in any major decisions. Like new schools or medical procedures."

"Okay. Sure." What was going on here?

"It's important to me."

"I promise, Hoyt. I'll call. We'll talk."

He seemed satisfied. "I realize we need to take things slow. For Benjie's sake, as well as ours. I won't push you into anything you aren't ready for or threaten a custody battle if you don't agree."

"I appreciate that."

"We're a team, and Benjie isn't a battleground."

He was saying all the right things, though his speech sounded a bit rehearsed. She wished she felt more confident.

A nudge in the arm from the horse reminded her she'd been shirking her duties. Dropping the brush in the nearby plastic caddy, she wiped her hands on her jeans.

"We have to leave soon for dinner," she said. "See you in the morning?"

"Wait. There's one more thing."

His tone gave her pause. More than that, it alarmed her. "What?"

"Is something going on with you and Shane?"

"I don't understand."

"I'm not blind, Cassidy. Or stupid."

"What did he say?"

"Nothing yet. I'm asking you first. Are you dating?"

Cassidy tried not to panic. "We're friends."

"Good friends?"

"Hoyt, nothing and no one is more important to me than Benjie. You don't need to worry."

"Relax. I'm not angry, Cassidy."

She stared at him. "You're not?"

"If any man other than me is going to be involved with my son, I'd rather it be Shane."

Wow. Did Hoyt just say he approved of her and Shane dating, or was this a test?

"Nothing's decided yet."

"I'd better get back. Told Benjie I'd watch the roping clinic with him."

After Hoyt left, Cassidy walked the horse to the row of outdoor stalls behind the main barn. The thirsty gelding buried his face in the automatic waterer and drank lustily. Cassidy rested her arms on the stall railing and watched, not quite ready to return to the arena.

Hoyt seemed to be saying he wouldn't fight her when it came to custody of Benjie. That might not stop Benjie from choosing to live with Hoyt when he was older like Ryder had. Her brother claimed he'd left because of loyalty to their dad. Was there another reason? Their mother, specifically, and her controlling nature?

Cassidy had always sided with their mother, in large part to justify the guilt she felt. Ryder, however, didn't know about her guilt. What if he'd left because of their mother's constant and chronic negativity toward their father?

That would *not* happen to her, Cassidy vowed. She'd try her hardest to speak well of Hoyt in front of Benjie and never put her son in a situation where he felt he had to pick one parent over the other.

While far from completely relieved, some of the tension left her.

"What's that? Another smile? This is becoming a habit."

Shane. He was here. Perhaps he'd come looking for her.

She faced him. "Thought you'd be at the roping clinic."

It was good to see him, and not just because of their mutual attraction. He'd also become her friend. Advising her and supporting her with Hoyt and Benjie and, in a small way, her father.

No man had done that for her. Not that she'd have let them. Only Shane. What, if any, significance did that have?

"Just came from the bulls," he said. "Your dad and I decided on a breeding schedule."

"You're making progress."

"And it gives me the rest of the day off."

"I was also thinking of taking a little time for myself." In truth, she'd been considering a long, hot bath.

"Why don't we spend it together? We could have dinner."

A date. She should have seen this coming.

It was on the tip of her tongue to refuse. She'd insisted there could be nothing between them until her personal life was sorted and settled. Then again, wasn't it? More or less, anyway.

All of a sudden, she wanted to forget her worries and enjoy herself for one night. What would be the harm? None. She and Shane were both single. Benjie adored him, and her family liked him. If Hoyt was bothered for any reason, he'd simply have to get over it.

"Sure."

Shane drew back, studying her intently. "Did you actually accept?"

"I did." She laughed.

"And here I was prepared to twist your arm."

"Life is full of surprises."

"It most certainly is." His gaze locked with hers and held. Cassidy broke away first. "Where are we going? I'll have to change clothes first." She tugged on the hem of her denim jacket.

"The Hole in the Wall has never-ending shrimp baskets on Saturday evenings."

While known more for its live bands and dancing than its cuisine, the honky-tonk did serve up decent specials.

"I haven't been there in ages." She honestly couldn't remember the last time.

"Pick you up at six?"

It was nearly four. She had plenty of time to get ready and…take a bath. Heavens, wouldn't that be a treat?

"Let me find Tatum. See if she can babysit Benjie tonight."

Cassidy hadn't planned on calling in her favor this soon. Hopefully, her friend was available.

Shane nodded. "See you at six."

She half expected him to kiss her. She fully expected him to give her a quick hug. He did neither before heading to his trailer, leaving her more than a little anxious about what to expect tonight.

The nerves Cassidy had been fighting to control were back with a vengeance. This time she wasn't afraid of what the future held. She was ready to embrace it.

SHANE WASN'T MUCH of a dancer. Or maybe he was, and the bodies bumping and jostling them from all sides affected his skills. Cassidy couldn't have cared less. She was enjoying herself simply being held snug in his arms.

Talk was impossible over the noise, and they'd all but given up trying. Of the three saloons in town, the Hole in the Wall was typically the place to be on weekends, due in large part to the band and food. While Cassidy and Shane were waiting for their orders to arrive, he'd asked her to dance. She'd accepted, acutely self-conscious about her own lack of skill when it came to tripping the light fantastic.

Too soon the music came to a stop, and Shane guided her through the throng of patrons to their table.

"Come here much?" he asked. From someone else, the question might have been a cheesy pickup line.

"Not really." Cassidy had to practically shout to be heard. "Once in a while Liberty used to drag me. Thanks to Deacon, those days are over."

"You don't sound sorry."

"The bar scene isn't exactly my thing."

"It goes with the territory."

That was true. Cowboys liked to whoop it up at the local hangouts almost as much as they did rodeoing. She was lucky to avoid the Hole in the Wall at all.

Tonight, it seemed, she didn't mind the noise and the crowd and the carrying on. Not with Shane for company.

"You must have been in your share of bars." She flashed him a smile, then caught herself. Had she just insulted him by implying he spent a lot of time partying?

"More than I care to count." He didn't appear offended, but with all the commotion surrounding them, it was hard to tell. "Like you, those days are over. Bria keeps me on the straight and narrow."

"Same for me. Because of Benjie."

He raised his long-neck bottle of beer. "First one of these I've had in a while. And it'll be my last one tonight."

She appreciated his concern for her feelings regarding drinking and driving. "Me, too."

"Then here's to living it up." He clinked his bottle against hers.

A few minutes later, the waitress arrived with their food. Before the woman could set down the shrimp baskets, Shane stopped her.

"Any chance we could take these outside?"

"Absolutely. There's plenty of seating."

"It'll be quieter," he told Cassidy as they followed the waitress through the patio entrance.

And colder, she thought, slipping into her jacket. What was Shane thinking?

Turned out, his idea was a perfect one. Besides being quieter and cozier than inside, the patio's freestanding gas heaters kept the area toasty warm. No sooner were they seated and the waitress gone than Cassidy removed her jacket.

"You were right to suggest this." She looked around. The tables were close, but not so close she worried their nearest neighbors would overhear their conversation.

"Better than inside. Though, I kind of liked the dancing."

"Me, too."

Shane grinned and dug into his basket, drowning a plump shrimp in cocktail sauce before popping it into his mouth.

She followed suit and tried to remember her last meal out that wasn't fast food or pizza. The shrimp practically melted in her mouth.

"Thank you," she said, a satisfied sigh escaping.

"I'm free tomorrow night, too."

She hesitated. "Maybe we should take this one step at a time."

"Whatever you're comfortable with."

Cassidy wouldn't agree to a second date until she saw how this one ended. She and Shane faced a lot of twists and curves in their relationship.

Strains of music floated through the partially open door, adding a delightful ambiance to their dinner. Conversation flowed. Cassidy couldn't recall talking this much ever. She regaled Shane with tales of Benjie growing up, wanting him to get to know his nephew better.

She stopped cold when he said, "Hoyt would love to hear that story. You should tell him."

Hoyt probably would love it, but she didn't enjoy the same sense of ease with him she did Shane. Perhaps she eventually would, with time and practice.

"Did he mention anything about us going out?" she asked.

"Earlier."

"And?"

"We talked more about how our lives are the same. Both of us having children we didn't know about."

"I suppose it is strange."

Shane smiled. "He's okay with us dating."

She gave a small shrug.

"You don't believe him?"

"If we were to…continue seeing each other, you'd be spending more time with Benjie than he would."

"I'm already spending more time with Benjie than Hoyt."

"As his uncle. Not as his mother's…"

"Boyfriend?" Shane finished for her, amusement lighting his features.

"Well, yes." And if things between them were to develop into more—not that she'd considered it, they'd barely had one date—the situation could become more complex.

"Guess we'll find out for sure soon enough." He sent her a look that warmed her inside and out, far more than the nearby gas heaters.

"One step at a time," she reminded him.

The band broke into a new number, this one a slow and romantic favorite of Cassidy's. Shane stood and reached out his hand to her.

"Dance with me."

She wasn't ready to leave the patio. "I like it out here."

"Who says we're going inside?"

He led her to an open area near the low stucco wall. She noticed the smiles and glances of the other diners. One woman jabbed her companion in the side and pointed at them as if to say, "Look at him. Now there's a guy with swagger."

A dozen steps into the dance, Cassidy realized she'd been wrong about Shane. With room to move, he proved to be a good dancer and expertly executed turns as they swayed to the music.

What else was he good at? Her mind wandered, venturing into territory she was hesitant to consider. With his palm pressed firmly into the small of her back and his lips brushing the hair at her temple, her mind wandered further.

When the song ended, she was tempted to ask him for another. The band announcing a short break put a stop to her plans.

"Another round of beer?" the waitress asked when she came to clear their table.

"Not for me," Cassidy said. "Thanks."

"Coffee?" Shane asked.

If she had a cup this late, she'd be up half the night. On the plus side, she could spend more time with Shane.

"Yes, please."

"Make it two," he told the waitress.

When they finally left forty minutes later, Cassidy was practically walking on air. For an entire evening, she'd forgotten all about her problems and simply enjoyed herself. Who'd have thought it possible? And why hadn't she done it sooner?

Hands clasped, they crossed the parking lot. The glow of the lights alternately cast Shane's face in shadows and light. The effect was intriguing. Halfway to his truck, he put his arm around her waist and pulled her snug against him.

"Cold?"

She hadn't been. Then again, she didn't want to give him reason to release her. "A little."

His arm stayed firmly in place.

"Thanks again for dinner," she said. "It was wonderful. The food and getting away."

"My pleasure."

His low, silky tone let her know the evening had indeed been pleasurable for him. At his truck, he opened the passenger door for her and waited as she climbed in. She was a bit disappointed he didn't try to kiss her. Her second strikeout that day. She tried telling herself it was for the best. She'd been the one, after all, to remind him repeatedly she wanted to proceed slowly.

"We could stop for dessert," he suggested as they drove past the Flat Iron, the town's iconic restaurant.

"I'm stuffed. But if you want to." Another excuse to prolong the date.

"Let's save that for next time."

Darn it. They were going home, a fact becoming increasingly apparent when he took the road leading to the arena.

"You okay?"

She glanced at him across the front seat. "Fine."

"You seem awfully quiet."

"Am I? Sorry."

She hadn't spoken for the last five minutes. Anxiety was getting the best of her. How was the date going to end? Was she wrong to put the brakes on earlier? Up until now, Shane had had no reservations about initiating their kisses.

"I had a great time." Even his smile wasn't its usual one-thousand-watt brightness.

"Me, too."

He pulled to a stop in front of her house and reached for his door handle. "I'll walk you to the door."

Then what? A kiss good-night? At that precise moment, the back porch light turned on. Her mother must have heard the truck engine. No way could Cassidy kiss Shane with her mother twenty feet away on the other side of the wall. If he intended to kiss her at all, considering how strangely he was acting.

"Wait!" she blurted.

His hand paused on the handle.

"Um." Had she lost her senses? "Can we…" Oh, jeez. She was insane. Or a fool. Both, in all likelihood.

"What, Cassidy?"

She wished she could see his face. Read his expression. Then, she'd know what to say next. But the interior of the truck was too dark.

"Can we go to your trailer? Just to talk," she clarified. "For a while. I'm not ready to call it a night." Was this what one beer and a basket of fried shrimp did to her? Turned her into someone who invited themselves inside a man's home? "Unless you're tired."

"I'm not tired." He threw the truck into Reverse.

As they passed beneath the arena's security light high atop a post, she saw his wide, satisfied grin.

Dammit! She'd been played. He'd wanted her to be the one to ask.

Cassidy squared her shoulders, not bemoaning the loss of her pride. Played or not, she wanted to be alone with Shane.

He unlocked the trailer door and waited for her to enter first. She hesitated before climbing the steps, remembering the last time she'd been here and their smoking hot kiss, rivaled only by the one on the bleachers. She was, she admitted, ready for another.

Wow, she barely recognized herself. This wasn't how

she behaved. Shane had completely changed not just her life but *her*. He'd given her courage. Filled the large empty void surrounding her heart. Taught her to let go of what wasn't important while still holding on to what was.

It was on the tip of her tongue to tell him how much he'd come to mean to her, but she couldn't.

"Cassidy?" Shane switched on the dim kitchen light. "Is something wrong?"

"Yes," she whispered and raised her hand to cup his strong jaw. "We're not doing this." Standing on tiptoes, she pressed her lips to his.

The kiss was sweet. Chaste. And all too brief. On a scale of one to ten, his response was maybe a one-point-five.

What an idiot she'd been, thinking he wanted her. Well, she wouldn't make that mistake again.

"Sorry," she muttered and spun, ready to flee.

"Don't go."

"I've made a terrible mistake."

"If you think that, then go ahead. Leave right now. Because if you don't, I'm going to kiss you again. *Really* kiss you this time."

Cassidy didn't move, except to part her lips in anticipation.

"Exactly what I thought," he said and wrapped her in his arms. When his mouth crashed down on hers, she was ready. And willing.

Chapter Twelve

More than once, Shane had cursed the trailer's cramped bedroom. He stubbed his toes on the corner of the dresser. Banged his elbows into the wall. Repeatedly walked into the closet door, which never quite closed all the way.

Tonight, he was grateful for the tight quarters, which put him close to Cassidy, and for the wall lamp with its low-energy bulb that emitted just the right amount of minimal light.

It hadn't been easy breaking down her defenses. Finally, with a lot of effort and double the patience, he'd succeeded. His reward was the passionate, sexy woman he'd glimpsed hidden beneath the surface.

She returned his kisses with a fervor matched by his own. It had been she who entered the trailer first, peeling off her jacket as she did. Then, when he'd unzipped his vest, she'd insisted on divesting him of it. Now, she tackled the buttons on his shirt.

"Whoa, sweetheart." He stayed her hands by taking them in his.

"Sorry," she murmured, her cheeks blushing a lovely pink.

"Don't be." Tucking a lock of hair behind her ear, he lifted her face to his. "I liked your enthusiasm. More than you can imagine. But I'd also like the night to last."

She smiled shyly, which was a charming contrast to her earlier unabashed eagerness. "I'm probably woefully out of practice. Which, I'm sure, the last five minutes demonstrated."

He bent his head and skimmed his lips along the side of her neck, paying special attention to the delicate skin beneath her jaw. She shuddered when he nibbled on her earlobe.

"Follow your instincts," he whispered, his voice rough with desire, "and we'll both be just fine."

She grabbed the front of her shirt and tugged, popping open the snaps in quick succession. Shane's eyes widened, at her lack of restraint and at the glorious sight before him. Beneath the lacy peach bra were a pair of beautifully rounded breasts, the loveliest he'd ever seen.

"Aw, hell," he said and scooped her up, one arm behind her knees, the other supporting her back. Walking to the bed, he deposited her in the middle. "Going slow has always been overrated."

With a low, sexy chuckle, she fell back onto the mattress. Shane swallowed, his throat sudden dry, and he lowered himself on top of her. The next instant, they were right where he wanted them to be, amid a tangle of arms and legs.

"My boots," she protested and toed them off. With a hollow thud, they fell to the trailer floor.

Shane did the same with his, then removed his shirt, nearly shredding the fabric in his haste. His white T-shirt came next.

"Oh, my." Cassidy stared at his bare chest with a look akin to wonder, then trailed her fingertips down the length of him, from collarbone to belt buckle. He hissed, his muscles clenching in response as her nails lightly scraped his skin.

"Sweetheart." He groaned when she unfastened his belt buckle. "I thought it was my turn to undress you."

She slid down his zipper. "Or you can watch me undress myself when I'm done here."

No man in his right mind could pass up an offer like that.

He wound up having to help her with his jeans, and was happy to oblige. She sat back on her calves while he removed his socks. Hooking his thumbs into the waistband of his briefs, he started to tug.

"No, let me," she said with relish and took over the task, easing the briefs over his hips. Her heated gaze lingered.

Shane was no Adonis, not in his opinion, anyway. But, thanks to years of hard, demanding labor, he knew he could hold his own in the physically fit department.

"My turn." He sat up and reached for her.

She withdrew. "That's not what we agreed on."

No, it wasn't. She'd promised to make all his dreams a reality.

Standing, she removed her shirt, fully exposing her peach bra and all her lovely bare skin. Next, she shimmied out of her jeans and tossed them onto the floor. In the pale light of the wall lamp, wearing no more than her underwear, she resembled a golden goddess. Shane had never been more enamored.

"You're incredible."

Her gaze softened. "You make me feel that way."

He fitted his hands to her waist and pulled her forward until she stood between his knees. Next, he skimmed his hands up her rib cage, stopping just shy of her breasts.

She slipped the bra straps off her shoulders. A moment later, the flimsy piece of lingerie lay on the floor beside her jeans.

Shane could only stare, unable to remember ever seeing, much less holding, such beauty. His hands were on the verge of shaking as he raised them to her breasts. The nipples instantly beaded at his touch. What would they taste like? He couldn't wait to find out.

He brought his mouth to first one breast, then the other, sucking greedily. Her breathing quickened. His was coming in great, loud rasps that filled his ears.

Oh, yeah. He'd been right, she tasted as delicious as she looked.

She threaded her fingers into his hair and kissed him soundly. "Make love to me, Shane."

"Count on it."

"Now."

He tugged on her bikini panties, sliding them down the length of her long, shapely legs. Once she stepped out of the skimpy garment, he ran his hands back up the same path. Her skin was like silk. He didn't want to stop.

Circling her waist with one arm, he pressed his splayed fingers to her belly. Like her breasts, the skin there was smooth as satin. Did it, too, taste delicious?

Shane found out for himself. She inhaled sharply as his mouth replaced his fingers. Trembled when his tongue circled her belly button. Not stopping there, he dipped his tongue inside, causing her to shudder.

"That tickles." She attempted to wriggle away from him.

He held fast, his arm circling her waist. "What about this?" He slipped his hand between her thighs and nearly lost it when he encountered her moist folds.

Her answer was a low, desperate moan.

She wanted him. As much as he wanted her. The knowledge excited him further.

Growing bolder, he slid a finger inside her. Then a second.

"Oh, Shane." Her limbs trembled, and she swayed unsteadily. "This is…"

"Incredible?"

She braced her hands on his shoulders and rocked her hips in rhythm with his thrusting fingers. "I was thinking indecent."

"Want me to stop?" He rubbed his thumb over her most sensitive spot.

Her eyes drifted closed.

"Yes?" He increased the pressure. "Or no?"

"Don't…stop." Her grip tightened, her nails digging into his flesh. "Please."

Taking his cues from her, he stroked and fondled and caressed her. She was incredible to watch, unbelievably responsive. He couldn't take his eyes from her expressive face. A moment later, she rewarded him, her body quivering as a stunning climax claimed her.

"Shane!" She threw back her head and gave herself over to the sensations.

He steadied her, not removing his hand until the tremors subsided and her legs grew stronger.

She exhaled a long, uneven breath. "Wow."

"My sentiments exactly."

"I don't usually… I haven't ever let a man…" She smiled shyly down at him, brushing the hair off his forehead. "I'm glad it was you."

The sincerity in her voice and the warmth in her eyes caused his chest to swell. She wasn't playing to his ego or feeding him a line. Her enjoyment had been genuine and real and, for him, just the beginning.

"Cassidy, this isn't a casual hookup. I care about you. A lot. I hope you know that."

When her gaze met his, he saw understanding blaze in her dark eyes. "I do."

"Our date tonight, it's the first of many."

"Maybe we can take the kids along with us sometime."

She was truly out to win his heart. "Sounds great."

Assuming she needed a few minutes to recoup, he was surprised—and delighted—when she pushed him down onto the bed and straddled his hips.

"Wait." He grabbed her hips and anchored her in place. "We can't yet. Not without protection."

"You're right." She nodded thoughtfully. "Do you have any?"

Shane almost laughed. She'd asked the question with the same nonchalance she might have when inquiring about the weather or his day at work. Would she ever cease to amaze him?

"There's some in the drawer." He reached for the built-in night stand.

She eyed him wryly. "You planned this?"

"No, no. Not at all." He faltered, realizing nothing he said would make him sound less of a heel. "They're left over from…" He was making this worse by the second.

"It's okay." She bent over him until their foreheads were touching. "I'm not upset." She kissed him, slow and sweet and thoroughly. It quickly escalated to fire and heat. "Now, Shane," she whispered when they broke apart, their former sensual mood restored. "I'm not sure I can wait any longer."

Damned if she wasn't the most extraordinary woman. Quickly donning the condom, he positioned her above him and drove inside. Incredible. Smooth. Slick. Tight. His body bucked involuntarily as sensations overpowered him.

Her moan of pure delight incited him to thrust deeper and harder. Within seconds, sweat broke out on his skin, as much from forcing himself to hold back as the physical exertion.

She shifted, the new position allowing him to go deeper,

feel more, give her greater pleasure. He ground his teeth together, unable to take much more. Filling his hands with her breasts, he squeezed and fondled.

After that, there was no going back and no stopping. His release came with all the force of a thundering stampede. He was aware of calling out her name. Of holding on to her as if he didn't dare let her go. Of needing her with a desperation exceeding all others. Ever.

When their breathing returned to a semblance of normal, she fell onto his chest, limp as a rag doll and completely spent. He, too, had yet to recover and might never.

"That was…pretty great," she said at last, dropping light kisses on his face and neck.

"Pretty?" Shane might have laughed if he wasn't exhausted. "Speaking for myself, I'll never be the same again."

She rose, her smile conveying just how aware she was of her effect on him. "I think we did okay for two people out of practice."

"We did great." He was already imagining the next time. Possibly later tonight.

When she went to roll off him, he pulled her down onto the mattress beside him.

"I should go," she murmured.

"Why?" He stroked the length of her back, familiarizing himself with the exquisite contours of her body. Round, lush hips. Narrow waist. Flat belly. Full breasts. She might not realize it, but she was made for a man's touch. His touch. "Isn't Benjie staying at Tatum's tonight?"

"My mom will notice I'm gone."

"Your mom's busy with your dad. He told me earlier they were having dinner together. He's at the house now."

"Ah." She made a wry face. "Now I understand the porch light."

"Didn't you see his truck?"

"I guess not."

"You okay with that? Your dad staying over?"

He felt her relax. "I'm better these days than I was."

"Good."

"Yeah." She stretched and sighed contentedly. "It is."

Shane had heard from Mercer that he and Cassidy had a heart-to-heart talk earlier today. His boss was of the opinion he and his daughter had rebuilt all their burned bridges. She seemed to share that opinion, to a degree anyway.

Shane was much more interested in the two of them than in Cassidy's parents.

"Stay with me tonight." He propped himself up on one elbow in order to gaze down at her. "I can't let you go."

"Can't?" she asked playfully.

"I'm serious. You're necessary to me and what we just had together, well, it doesn't happen often. Never to me. And I don't want it to end."

"If I stay here, my family will find out."

"I'll speak to them. Let them know my intentions are honorable."

"Honorable, huh?" She grinned and nestled closer.

"I'd like to see where this leads. I have a chance to make a real life for myself and Bria here in Reckless. I'm thinking I'd like that life to include you and Benjie."

Her expression softened. "I'd like to see where this leads, too. But I should warn you. I'm not the easiest person to get along with, even on my good days."

"Sweetheart, I wouldn't have you any other way."

Shane kissed her then. A moment later, when the smoldering embers between them had been stoked into a fiery blaze, he pressed her onto her back and covered her body with his.

She was spending the night with him. He wouldn't

take no for an answer. And in the morning, they'd make plans for the day, and the next day and the one after that.

"Do tell." Liberty's eyes lit up.

"There's nothing to tell." Cassidy dismissed her sister with a nonchalant wave. Inside, she was still tingling from Shane's good morning kisses.

"You spent the night with him!"

"Technically, two nights."

Liberty gasped with delight. "Details. I demand details."

Cassidy obliged her sister by summarizing the first night with Shane after the trail ride. Luckily, Benjie had yet to wake, giving the sisters some time alone.

"It's been incredible. Yesterday, while Hoyt took Benjie to the Phoenix Zoo, Shane and I went on a drive in the mountains. On the way home, we stopped in Punkin Center for dinner. I haven't been there in years."

"That's all?"

Cassidy grinned slyly. "All I'm telling."

Parting from Shane last night had been hard. Which was why, after Benjie had gone to bed, Cassidy had slipped out to his trailer, then hurried back to the house before anyone was awake. Liberty, at the arena earlier than usual, had caught sight of Cassidy and confronted her in the kitchen a few minutes ago.

"Not one juicy tidbit?" Liberty implored. "You're mean."

At that moment, their mother stumbled into the kitchen, took one look at Cassidy and announced, "Didn't you sleep? You look terrible."

"Me?"

With her hair in complete disarray, her robe hanging off her left shoulder and dark shadows beneath her eyes, her mother wasn't one to talk.

"Dad spent the night," Liberty said.

"Again?" Cassidy raised an eyebrow.

Her mother huffed defensively. "People in glass houses have no right to judge."

Cassidy rolled her eyes. "That's not how the saying goes, Mom." She grabbed a mug from the cupboard. After pouring herself some coffee, she joined her mother and sister at the table. "Fine. I'm seeing Shane. You care to comment?"

Liberty beamed at their mother. "I totally saw this coming."

Cassidy refrained from commenting. Her younger sister was head over heels in love and soon to be married. As a result, she imagined all sorts of romantic pairings, some with the most unlikely of couples.

"I'm happy for you, darling." Her mother patted Cassidy's hand.

The reassuring gesture didn't fool Cassidy. She knew her mother well enough to detect "the tone."

"What's wrong, Mom?"

"Nothing."

"Come on. Tell me."

"I simply think you should be careful."

"Are you kidding?" Liberty gaped at their mother, clearly appalled. "Shane's a great guy. He's settled, a family man, ready to make his home in Reckless and the best bull manager in six states. Not to mention gorgeous. She could do a whole lot worse."

"His brother is also Benjie's father."

"Don't think we haven't considered that." Cassidy and Shane had done more than while away the hours snuggled under the covers. They'd talked at great length about all sorts of things, including Shane's relationship with Benjie and the trials they faced. "We understand it's complicated, and we're treading carefully."

"Spending every night with him isn't treading carefully."

"Two nights." Cassidy's hackles rose. She wanted her mother to be glad for her. Not deliver her a lecture.

"Besides," Liberty added, "it's not like you and Dad have an uncomplicated relationship."

"And you're suddenly an expert?" Their mother glowered at her.

Liberty frowned. "It's true. You divorced him years ago, lied to him, refused to allow him in our lives. Then, he returns, practically forces you to accept him as your business partner—"

"No practically about it," Cassidy interjected.

"Right. And now he's courting you, telling everyone you're getting married again." Liberty snorted. "Cassidy and Shane don't even compare."

"We're not getting married." Their mother turned away to reknot her bathrobe belt.

The sisters exchanged glances. Something was amiss.

"What happened?" Liberty asked.

"Nothing." Their mother's answer rang false.

"Did you and dad have another fight?" Liberty persisted.

"No."

"Is he drinking again?" Cassidy asked.

"Jeez, Cassidy, why do you always assume the worst?" Her mother made a visible effort to control her emotions.

Okay, maybe she wasn't being fair. She tended to jump to conclusions where her father was concerned. "You're right. I shouldn't have said that. Old habits are hard to break."

"He loves you so much, honey. Both of his girls." Their mother's gaze traveled from Cassidy to her sister. "And he wants what's best for you."

"We have the best," Liberty said. "Deacon and Shane."

Cassidy agreed wholeheartedly.

Was this what it was like to be in love? Believe one had the best? Truthfully, Cassidy didn't know the answer. She hadn't been in love before. Not really. Not the way her sister was in love. Cassidy had had a small taste with Hoyt. She'd cared greatly for him, but not enough to try harder when, after six months, their relationship deteriorated.

In hindsight, she probably should have broken up with him sooner. But then she wouldn't have Benjie.

"So what's wrong?" Liberty demanded.

Their mother tiredly swirled her coffee. "We were up late talking is all."

"About getting married?"

"I'm just not ready."

The kitchen door swinging open made the three of them simultaneously turn their heads. Ryder strode in, looking recently showered and shaved. He was wearing a freshly pressed Western shirt.

Their mother instantly brightened. "Good morning. You must have a meeting today."

Like the rest of them, he went straight for the coffee-maker on the counter and poured himself a cup. "Actually, Tatum and I have an appointment with Pastor Douglas at the Guiding Light Community Church."

Their mother jumped up from her chair. "You're changing the wedding date?"

"Well, it depends on whether or not the church is booked. We're looking at April."

"That's two months away!" Her hand flew to her heart. "How can we possibly plan a second wedding in such a short amount of a time? Liberty's getting married in August."

"Don't worry, Mom. It's going to be a small, intimate service. Family and a few close friends." He gave Liberty's shoulders a squeeze. "As long as you and Deacon are okay with it. We don't want to steal your thunder."

Cassidy resisted rolling her eyes. Liberty was planning a wedding the likes of which Reckless had never seen.

"Are you kidding?" Liberty returned the hug. "I'm thrilled. Tatum's a wonderful woman, and she has three of the cutest kids."

All at once, everything fell into place, and Cassidy blurted, "Tatum's pregnant."

Their mother grabbed Ryder and shook him, her feet dancing in place. "Is that true?"

He grinned sheepishly. "She took the home pregnancy test yesterday."

"Oh, my God! I'm so excited for you both." She pulled him into a fierce bear hug. "Another grandchild." Tears filled her eyes.

Cassidy wanted to cry a little herself. Only a short time ago, the rift in her family had seemed too wide to ever bridge. Now, they were growing by yet another member.

"Tatum wanted to tell you herself," Ryder said to Cassidy after their mother finally released him. "I owe you an apology for letting the cat out of the bag."

"It's all right. You deserve to be excited."

"I am."

She could tell. Her brother wore the look of a man completely over the moon. Her own heart was ready to burst.

More hugs were exchanged and tears of joy wiped away. Cassidy, unfortunately, was jarred out of the sentimental moment by her cell phone ringing down the hall.

"Excuse me." Thinking it might be Tatum about the pregnancy news, or Shane checking on her, she dashed to her bedroom. It was neither of them. Instead, Hoyt's number appeared on the display. Had he and Cheryl changed their minds about visiting this morning to say goodbye to Benjie? Had Shane told Hoyt about their last two nights together?

No, impossible. She and Shane had decided to wait until after Hoyt and Cheryl left. Why potentially rock the boat?

She answered the call with a breathless and slightly anxious, "Hello."

"Morning. Did I wake you?"

"No, I'm always up early." Very early this morning. "Are you still coming by?"

"We're on our way now."

"Um, Benjie's still asleep. I'll wake him and get him fed and dressed."

"No hurry."

That was odd. Hoyt and Cheryl didn't have long before they needed to leave for the airport.

"I'd like to talk to you," Hoyt said.

"What about?"

There was a long pause during which Cassidy imagined the worst. Finally, when she could stand no more, Hoyt said, "I want more time with Benjie."

Her pulse instantly raced. "This coming summer?"

"No. Starting right now. Today."

"Wait. You're leaving in a few hours."

"We postponed our flight and are taking the redeye tonight."

"Why?" Something more was going on, and her panic escalated.

"I've been talking to Cheryl and Shane. They're both in agreement."

"Shane? What does he have to do with this?"

"It was his idea, actually. He suggested we stay another day in Reckless and that I talk to Benjie about additional visitation. Possibly taking him for the entire summer."

Cassidy swayed, feeling as if she'd been shoved from behind. This couldn't be happening to her. Benjie was slipping through her fingers, and Shane was the one responsible.

Chapter Thirteen

"I can't let you do you that." Cassidy shook her head.

"You're not in sole charge of Benjie. Not anymore." Hoyt spoke tersely through clenched teeth.

They'd been bickering nonstop for the past fifteen minutes, and he was clearly losing patience with her.

"I don't mind you wanting to take Benjie fishing before you leave." The truth was, she did mind, but she was trying her best to be accommodating. "What I do mind is you and him scheduling additional visitation without me present."

"He'll respond better if you're not there."

"You mean you can manipulate him more easily."

"Don't make me out to be the bad guy, Cassidy. I'm the one who went six years with no idea I had a son."

Okay, she had hit a little below the belt. "I'm sorry. That was uncalled-for."

Hoyt didn't acknowledge her apology. "I'm his father. I have rights."

"You do, but those rights don't include you getting to come here and make outrageous demands."

"Seeing Benjie isn't outrageous."

"He's too young to understand and far too young to make his own decisions. Of course he'll agree to additional visitation. He's excited to have a father."

"No more excited than I am to have a son."

"Enough with laying on the guilt."

She and Hoyt sat at the picnic table in the backyard, not far from where she and Shane had argued at Benjie's birthday party. Funny how things came full circle.

Cheryl waited inside the house with Benjie and Sunny, who'd volunteered to keep Cheryl company and oversee Benjie's breakfast so Cassidy and Hoyt could talk in private.

Cassidy rubbed her temples. "We agreed to let the attorneys hammer out the schedule."

"Actually, *you* told me how it was going to be, and I didn't object." Hoyt sat opposite her, his crossed arms propped on the table. Everything about his demeanor and posture was confrontational. "Now, I've had time to think and process."

And talk to Shane. Cassidy was still in a state of shock from hearing the news. Whatever he'd said had caused his brother to change overnight.

She'd yet to confront Shane. There'd been no time, plus she was too angry and hurt. Mostly hurt. They'd spent the weekend together, for crying out loud. Made love. Discussed the future. Held each other for endless hours. Laughed, teased and simply sat in contented silence.

That he would influence Hoyt against her was like a betrayal of the worst kind. She simply didn't know what to make of it.

"Please, Hoyt. You can't spring this on me with no warning and expect me to go along."

"I'm taking Benjie fishing at the lake. Along with sports and school and whatever other subject comes up, we're going to discuss him coming to live with me for part of the year. I want to get a gauge for how he feels before meeting with my attorney."

Her heart stopped beating. "One minute ago it was the

entire summer. Now, you want him for part of the year. What's next?"

"The more you fight me," Hoyt said, "the more time with Benjie I'm going to demand. And when our attorneys get together, it'll be to discuss a custody suit."

"You promised not to threaten me."

"New terms, Cassidy."

Her head pounded, and her stomach roiled. Please, Lord, let this all be some sort of awful, horrible mistake.

"What do you want, Hoyt?" The scratchy voice was barely recognizable to her ears.

"What I've been telling you since I called. To take Benjie fishing."

When Hoyt had originally made the request, Cassidy deemed it completely out of the question. In light of this last demand, for shared custody, a drive to the lake was nothing.

"I need to make a call," she said feebly.

"Now?"

"Five minutes."

He grunted his consent, and Cassidy struggled to escape the picnic table that had become a trap. Going to stand by the modular play set, she removed her phone from her pocket and dialed her attorney. When the call went straight to voice mail, she hung up and dialed Deacon. Thankfully, he answered on the first ring.

"Hoyt wants to take Benjie fishing," Cassidy said, then filled him in on the specifics.

"What's the problem?"

"He plans on discussing additional visitation with Benjie. Naturally, Benjie will agree."

"Okay."

"Okay!" Cassidy squeaked, her anxiety rising by degrees. Sensing Hoyt's eyes on her, she turned her back to him. "He threatened me with a custody suit."

"Cassidy, calm down, will you?"

"I can't let him take Benjie from me."

"All I'm hearing is a fishing trip."

"To discuss visitation. Without me there."

"As long as it's not immoral or illegal, you can't dictate what he and Benjie talk about."

Her resolve to stay strong waned, and she swallowed a sob. "I'm scared. Benjie's young. And impressionable."

Deacon softened his voice. "Trust me when I say, don't fight Hoyt on this. His request isn't out of line."

"Custody! It's crazy. Insane."

"Taking Benjie fishing. The rest, at this point anyway, is Hoyt's temper getting the best of him. I wouldn't put a lot of stock in what he says."

"He seems pretty serious."

"This could be his way of testing you. To see how far he can push you. Your best defense is to remain calm."

"It's hard," she whispered.

"I know." Deacon stopped talking to her like an attorney and consoled her like a friend. "Hoyt's leaving today. He's emotional. Once he gets home, he may change his mind."

She glanced at Hoyt and was confronted by his implacable stare. "Somehow I doubt that."

"Hang in there, Cassidy, and save your strength. This is only the beginning."

After a few more words of encouragement, she and Deacon disconnected, and she returned to Hoyt.

"Well?" he demanded.

"Fine. Take Benjie for the morning." The painful lump in her throat made speaking difficult. "But swear to me you'll have him home by noon."

Hoyt didn't exactly smile, though the lines around his face become less rigid. "One o'clock at the latest."

It was, she supposed, the best she could hope for.

The back door banged open, and Benjie charged out. Breakfast was obviously over, and he could no longer be contained.

"Daddy." He ran straight for Hoyt. "Cheryl says we're going fishing."

Cassidy suppressed a scream of frustration. What business did Cheryl have telling Benjie before the decision was made?

In the span of an hour, her perfect world had spun out of control. First, Shane went behind her back to Hoyt. All right, maybe not behind her back, but he should have told her about his conversation with Hoyt. Then Hoyt showed up making demands and threatening her. Now, Cheryl had overstepped her bounds. It was too much all at once.

Hoyt lifted Benjie into his arms and held him against his chest. "You ready to give that new rod and reel of yours a trial run?"

"Yes!" Benjie cranked his head sideways to ask Cassidy, "Can I, Mom?"

"She's already agreed," Hoyt cut in before Cassidy could reply.

"Yes, you can." She wasn't about to let him speak for her. Or let Benjie think he could pit one parent against the other. "For a few hours. Remember, you have school tomorrow."

Just when she thought things couldn't get worse, Shane approached from the direction of the arena, not looking at all surprised to see his brother. Then again, as far as Cassidy knew, this entire trip to the lake was his idea. He'd mentioned taking Bria one day soon.

"Hi." He smiled warmly and dipped his head for a kiss. She deftly sidestepped him and, frowning, cut her glance to Benjie.

Shane must have figured out this wasn't the time or

place for a discussion because he said nothing. Fortunately, both Hoyt and Benjie appeared oblivious.

"Hi, Uncle Shane."

"Hey, partner." Shane waited until Hoyt set Benjie down, then ruffled the boy's hair, after which the two brothers clapped each other on the back. "You heading to the airport soon?"

Airport? Hadn't Shane heard?

"Cheryl called and booked us a later flight," Hoyt said. "I took your advice. She, Benjie and I are heading to the lake first for a little fishing."

"You are?"

"Last-minute decision."

"I see."

Either Shane didn't know about the trip or he was a great actor. What, then, was the advice he'd given his brother?

"Come with us," Hoyt invited.

Hold on a minute. He got to tag along and not Cassidy?

"Thanks." Shane caught her glance. "But I have plenty to do here."

Whatever he was planning wouldn't include her. Not after she told him how she felt about his interference.

"Speaking of which," Hoyt said, "we need to get going. It's already eight." He took Benjie's hand. "Where'd you put your new fishing pole?"

The two of them walked toward the house, Cassidy following—except she didn't get far. Shane stopped her by blocking her path.

"What's wrong?"

She gaped at him. "You have to ask?"

"Frankly, yes. A few hours ago, I was holding you naked in my bed and we were deciding whether you, me and Benjie were going out for pizza tonight or staying home and grilling hot dogs."

"Did you tell Hoyt to challenge me for custody?"

"Why would I do that?" He frowned in confusion. "He lives in Wyoming."

"Well, he's threatening to take me to court if I don't cooperate."

"Cooperate how?"

"Allow more visitation. Let him take Benjie for part of the year."

"Did you say no?"

She suppressed a groan. "It's not the visitation I object to. It's his methods. He insists on talking to Benjie alone. Without me. He *says* Benjie will be more receptive, but what he's doing is pitting Benjie against me."

"That doesn't sound like Hoyt."

"It's exactly like Hoyt. He bullied me when we were dating."

"Bullied is a pretty strong word."

"I'm not making this up."

"I admit, he can be overbearing."

"He said you and he talked and the fishing trip was your suggestion."

Shane shook his head. "That's not true."

"You suggested Hoyt take Benjie fishing on Saturday when he gave Benjie the rod and reel."

"Hoyt did call me this morning right after you left the trailer and asked about my custody arrangement with Judy."

"What did you tell him?"

"I said I value each moment I spend with my daughter and regret the missed years. I suggested he take advantage of every opportunity to see Benjie. All the rest, the fishing trip, visitation, the custody suit, is entirely his doing."

Cassidy supposed it was possible for Hoyt to have taken Shane's words and put his own twist on them. Or maybe Cheryl had influenced him.

"Look," Shane continued. "Hoyt is single-minded

when he wants something. The more you dig in your heels, the more he'll push. Give a little, and he'll give, too. Possibly back off entirely."

Deacon had said pretty much the same to Cassidy during their call.

"Do you really think that?"

Shane nodded. "I'll call him later. Talk some sense into him."

"Thank you." Hoyt did listen to Shane.

He put his arm around her, and she leaned into him rather than resist. He was looking out for her, after all. And, were she honest, she'd admit how good it felt to have someone special in her life to count on.

"This has me rattled," she said. "Hoyt keeps saying one thing and doing another."

"He's always been impetuous."

Benjie was a lot like that, too. Hardly began one task, and he was off to another.

Worst case, the lake wasn't far. If needed, she could drive there and get Benjie. Though, she was probably getting ahead of herself. Hoyt had promised they'd be home by one o'clock.

A terrifying thought occurred to her. "He won't be drinking, will he?" A lot of people imbibed while fishing. For some, the two were inseparable.

"No. Absolutely not."

"How can you be sure? He drank and drove when we were dating."

"He and Cheryl gave up alcohol when they started fertility treatments."

"They did?" She was relieved and impressed.

Shane pulled her into a warm hug. "I don't agree with the arm-twisting tactics he pulled on you. And while I did encourage him to spend more time with Benjie, it wasn't to hurt you."

"I know." She hugged him back.

"Come on." He pulled her along with him.

"Where?"

"The Dawn to Dusk Coffee Shop."

"I should get to work. I'm scheduled to teach a riding class in an hour."

"We have time for a caramel latte to go."

When it came to arm twisting, Hoyt had nothing on Shane.

He stopped and, cupping her cheek, bent to brush his lips across hers. "The next few hours are going to be rough for you. Coffee will help."

Her mouth dissolved into a smile. "Is this your idea of a bribe?"

He flashed her that sexy grin she'd grown to love. "It's my idea of what a boyfriend does for his girlfriend."

Coffee did hit the spot. Cassidy sailed through her first riding class. The second one, however, dragged. At eleven forty-five she concocted an excuse to leave the arena in order to be at the house when Benjie returned.

On the way, she ran into Shane. It pleased her to think he might be watching for her.

"You won't mind if I come by later?" he asked, giving her a quick kiss.

"Not at all." She lingered for a moment, enjoying the sensation of laying her head on his shoulder.

On the walk to the house, Cassidy dialed Hoyt's cell phone, assuming they were on their way, if not nearly home. It rang six times before going to voice mail. Frustrated, she shoved her phone back into her jacket pocket. Maybe they were out of range. Nearby Pinnacle Peak was notorious for interfering with reception.

Inside the house, she tackled their never lessening mountain of laundry. Every ten to fifteen minutes, she paused to call Hoyt. Each time he didn't answer, her frustration and anger increased, as did her worry. Why hadn't she asked for Cheryl's number, as well?

By one thirty, she'd abandoned the laundry and paced the house. Was it too soon to call the sheriff's department and report her son missing?

Finally, at two-fourteen exactly, and after a dozen attempted calls, Hoyt answered his phone.

Cassidy instantly laid into him. "Where the hell are you?"

"We're still at the marina."

"Is Benjie all right?"

"He's fine."

"I want to talk to him. Put him on the phone."

"Cassidy, for God's sake, will you calm down?"

"You swore you'd have him home by noon. One at the latest. Am I wrong, or don't you have a plane to catch?"

"There's been a change of plans," he said slowly.

"Another one?"

"Listen to me."

"Whatever it is, the answer's no." She would not allow him to do this to her a second time. They were establishing ground rules, and the first one was that he didn't get to run the show. "Benjie has homework to do for school tomorrow. He needs to come home."

Hoyt cleared his throat. "I've rented a boat. We're staying overnight on the lake. We won't be back until later tomorrow."

An incessant pounding on his trailer door had Shane leaving the water running in the sink to see who the heck was in such a hurry. He hoped there wasn't a problem with one of the bulls. Come to think of it, Wasabi had been hobbling a bit yesterday.

He'd barely turned the knob when the door was literally yanked from his hand. Cassidy stood there, jacketless, windblown and flushed.

"Hi, sweetheart."

Not waiting for an invitation, she climbed the steps and pushed past him into the trailer. "Your brother took Benjie."

"What!" Shock coursed through Shane. "You're kidding."

"He did." She faced him across the small space. Tears had left telltale smudges beneath her red, swollen eyes.

He quickly shut off the water, then took her in his arms, wishing he could erase her pain. "I'm sorry. I can see you're upset."

"With good reason." She pushed away from him and paced the small space.

"I agree. We'll straighten this out. Get Benjie back."

Frankly, Shane couldn't believe his ears. What was his brother thinking? Fishing was one thing, but leaving Reckless with Benjie, before he and Cassidy had reached a formal custody agreement…it was heartless and cruel. It would also hurt his case when the time came to appear before the judge.

Shane reached for his phone on the table, intending to call Hoyt. "They probably haven't boarded the plane yet. Their flight's not for another hour."

She stared at him, confusion clouding her features. "Plane? What are you talking about?"

"You said Hoyt took Benjie."

"He did."

"Aren't they on their way to the airport?"

"They're still at the lake." Cassidy's voice broke. "Hoyt rented a boat. They're staying overnight."

"At the lake." Shane let the information sink in. "Not the airport."

"Yes!" Cassidy resumed pacing. "Hoyt promised to have Benjie home by noon. I called and called and *called*. He didn't answer until after two. Then it was to tell me he was keeping Benjie. Whether I liked it or not."

"Look, I'm not defending Hoyt's tactics, so don't misunderstand me."

She halted midstep. "Don't say you're siding with him."

"Of course I'm not siding with him."

"Then why would I misunderstand you?"

"Calm down, and let's put this in perspective, okay? Benjie's all right." Shane paused. "He is all right, yes? You did talk to him?"

"Not at first. Hoyt wouldn't let me. We had a big fight, and then he finally put Benjie on."

"He shouldn't have done that. No question. But again, Benjie's fine, you know where he is and he'll be home tomorrow. Concentrate on those things."

"Hoyt *swore* he'd have Benjie home today. What guarantee do I have he won't pull the same stunt tomorrow?"

"He has a rodeo this coming weekend. And Cheryl works. They have to get home."

"And Benjie has school tomorrow, which he's going to miss."

"It's one day."

"That's not the point!"

"I understand you're angry, Cassidy. Hoyt was out of line. He put you through a lot of needless worry. But Benjie is also his son. A son he hardly knows. Wanting to spend more time with him is understandable. You could cut him some slack."

"Did you know he was planning on taking Benjie?"

Shane didn't like the accusation in her tone. "If I did, I'd have insisted he tell you."

"I'm sorry. I'm taking my frustration out on you." She buried her face in her hands. "I was just so worried. I still am."

"Hoyt won't let anything happen to Benjie."

"I just wish you hadn't encouraged him."

"Wait a minute." Shane straightened. "This isn't my fault."

"Hoyt was ready to leave today. Then, he talked to you."

"Benjie had a choice, too. Did you ask him if he wanted to spend the night with his father?"

"No."

"Was that because you didn't want to hear the answer?"

Her eyes widened, then narrowed. "The problem here is Hoyt," she snapped. "Not me or Benjie."

"There are two sides to every story."

"Implying what, exactly?"

"It's possible you're hanging on too tight to Benjie. Being too controlling."

She recoiled as if struck. "I'm no such thing."

"You're used to dictating Benjie's every action without having to consider anyone else. Now, there's Hoyt. It's a big change and will take some getting used to. Judy's going through the same growing pains with Bria and me."

"Have you ever taken Bria without Judy's permission?"

"We've already agreed Hoyt was wrong. Rehashing it won't solve the problem."

"What will?" She stabbed her chest with her thumb. "Me admitting I'm a control freak?"

He didn't react to her anger. "If you are, you come by it naturally. Didn't you tell me last night how, when your father first came back to Reckless, he strong-armed your mother and forced her to accept him as her business partner?"

"I am *nothing* like my father."

"You do like to be in charge."

"Hoyt broke his promise."

Shane swore he could see steam pouring from her ears. "Maybe he wouldn't have if he'd thought you'd listen to reason."

"I let him take Benjie. That was reasonable."

"Let him? Benjie isn't a possession."

As if collapsing from the inside, she stacked her hands on the table and laid her head down.

Shane could have kicked himself. In trying to get through to her, he'd been too harsh.

"You're choosing Hoyt over me," she said in a small, defeated voice.

"I'm not." Given the choice, he'd have sat next to her. Since there was no room, he slid into the other side of the table. "You've been holding on to Benjie so long and so fiercely, you don't know how to let go. Even a little."

"I don't want to let go. I'm afraid of what will happen."

Right. Her brother. "Did your mother ever let Ryder visit your dad?"

"Of course not." Her head shot up. "Dad was an alcoholic."

"Say he wasn't. Would your mom have let Ryder, and you, too, go to Kingman?"

"I…don't know. Maybe. But what difference does it make?"

"If you were to give Benjie a little freedom, he might not abandon you like Ryder did."

"There's a big difference between me giving Benjie freedom and Hoyt taking him," she snapped.

"I don't disagree. Simply making a suggestion."

"I could drive to the lake." Cassidy looked at him expectantly. "You could come with me."

Shane sat back. "Don't do that. You showing up unannounced will make matters worse."

"I just want to check on Benjie. Take him some things. He needs pajamas and a toothbrush and clean clothes for tomorrow."

"It won't hurt him to sleep in his clothes one night." Shane had done much worse during his rodeo days. "And I'm sure the marina store sells toothbrushes."

Cassidy wrung her hands. "Benjie's never been away

from home before, except for spending the night at Tatum's."

"Let it go, Cassidy."

She stared out the tiny trailer window into the darkness.

"How about I fix dinner here?" he said. "We'll go to bed early and start fresh in the morning after a good night's sleep."

She looked at him. "*You* could drive out there."

"I'm not." Seriously, enough was enough.

At his sharp reply, Cassidy sprang from the seat. "I thought you cared about me."

"I do. Which is why I've spent the last twenty minutes listening to you rant."

"Rant!"

"Sorry, wrong choice of words."

Her features crumbled. "I trusted you."

"I haven't let you down."

"You won't drive out to the lake."

"I would if there was a reason. But Benjie's fine."

"You're the first man I've let get close to me since Hoyt." She stiffened. "I thought you were different."

Shane's temper snapped. He'd been making allowances for her because she was under enormous stress. No more. "That's unfair and uncalled-for."

She narrowed her gaze. "Caring for someone means unconditional support."

"I do support you. And I'll talk to Hoyt. But I'm not going out to the lake like some crazed person and searching for them. Especially when I don't feel Hoyt's entirely at fault."

"And you think I am?"

He sighed. "This is arguing for the sake of arguing."

She whirled and headed for the door.

Well, she'd warned him about her stubborn streak. "Cassidy, don't go. Not like this."

"We're done."

Good idea. A cooling-off period might benefit them both.

"I'll call you later," he said. "Better yet, I'll come by the house."

"Don't bother." She stopped at the door. "I won't see you."

He didn't like the finality in her voice and crossed the small room in two steps. "Today? Or again?"

She refused to turn around.

"Cassidy."

"You're breaking my heart, Shane." She left without a backward glance.

He thought of going after her, but didn't, telling himself she was just being Cassidy. Instead, he returned to work, his way of coping with stress when climbing on the back of a bull wasn't available.

Despite her warning not to bother, Shane dropped by the house later to see Cassidy—twice. Once right before supper and once about eight o'clock. Both times, Sunny politely but coolly informed him Cassidy wasn't available.

He took the first rejection in stride. She was mad and needed some solitude and space. The second rejection annoyed him. He accepted that people occasionally fought. But in order to compromise, learn and coexist harmoniously, there had to be communication. His parents, happily married for nearly forty years, had taught him that.

During his second attempt to see her, he'd tried to enlist Sunny's aid, until she rebuffed him. Probably for the best. Who knew how much Cassidy had told Sunny, or how willing she was to be drawn into an argument that, as far as he was concerned, didn't involve her?

And, really, did he want her help? She'd treated Mercer poorly in the past. Shane would rather not receive the same treatment himself, thank you very much.

Face it, the Becketts were complicated people with a complicated past and who complicated their relationships as much as possible.

He should wise up and take warning from what had happened with Cassidy today. If every difference of opinion ended up like this one, with the boxing gloves out and her storming off, refusing to speak to him, they didn't have a snowball's chance in hell of making it to next week, much less long term.

Chapter Fourteen

After a final pass by the bull pens, something Shane did more to burn off excess energy than any real concern that the stock wasn't quietly settled in for the night, he wandered back to his trailer. It was nearing ten and sleep beckoned. The crack of dawn came early, and he had a full day tomorrow.

Instead of hitting the shower as was his habit, he grabbed a soda from the fridge and, sitting at the table, powered up his laptop. He and Bria had recently taken up a new daily routine of emailing each other pictures and jokes and sometimes a short note. It was a way of maintaining constant contact. It was good for both of them. Of course, the emails were sent to and from Judy's account, who read them to Bria and composed the ones from her to Shane.

He was pleased to find a new email from Bria in his inbox including the link to a humorous YouTube video. Smiling, he watched the video in the semidarkness before firing off a quick reply. The smile promptly dimmed as thoughts of Cassidy and their disagreement intruded.

She was an amazing person. A loving and devoted mother, a hard worker with an incredibly passionate nature that, when ignited by the right spark, was a wonder to behold. That same passion, unfortunately, could also take the form of anger, obstinacy and tunnel vision.

Life with her would never be boring. It would also be a challenge, and Shane had begun asking himself if he was up to the task.

It was possible they'd rushed into their relationship before either of them was ready. They were both still putting their lives in order. Shane had a new daughter and a new job. Cassidy had recently reconciled with her estranged brother and father. Wasn't tonight proof enough they were ill-prepared for the challenges facing them? One fight and Cassidy was ready to call it quits.

His chest tightened. She *had* called it quits. This was no cooling-off period. Two visits, four phone calls and three texts, all unanswered, couldn't be denied. The realization left him hollow inside.

Closing his laptop, he began getting ready for a shower and bed. His steps were slow, his spirits low. Foolishly, he'd hoped he and Cassidy could beat the odds. He should probably be glad to get out early before they hurt each other worse than they already had. Hadn't history shown them they didn't have what it took for the long haul? Heck, this time they hadn't even lasted a month.

Tired as he was, sleep eluded Shane. Quite a difference from the last two nights he'd spent with Cassidy. He hadn't slept then, but for entirely different reasons.

His ringing cell phone made Shane bolt upright in bed. He glanced at the alarm clock on the night stand, momentarily confused. Twenty past eleven? Apparently, he'd fallen asleep, after all.

The distinctive ring identified the caller as Hoyt.

"Hey," Shane cleared the sleep from his voice. "What's up?"

"It's Benjie." His brother didn't return the greeting. "He won't stop crying."

Shane didn't need to be told. He could hear Benjie's wails in the background. "Is he hurt?"

"No. I don't think so. He was fine up until a couple hours ago. We fished all afternoon, then had sandwiches from the marina store for dinner. I have no idea what's wrong."

"He could be sick."

"Cheryl felt his forehead. She doesn't think he has a temperature. And he's not throwing up."

"What did he eat besides sandwiches?"

"Fast food chicken at lunch with the usual fixings," Hoyt said.

"What else?"

"Chips and dip. Cupcakes. I bought him an ice cream bar at the marina store."

Not the healthiest of snacks. And consumed on a rocking boat. "You sure he doesn't have a stomachache?"

"He didn't say."

Shane felt like he was leading a toddler by the hand. Was he once that naive? "Ask him."

There was a rustling on the line while Hoyt put the phone down. He came back a minute later.

"No stomachache."

"What does he say is wrong?"

There was a long hesitation before his brother answered. "Something about being scared."

"Of what?" Shane heard it then, loud and crystal clear. Benjie cried out over and over that he wanted to go home and wanted his mother. "Want my advice? Take him home."

"You sure he won't quit and fall asleep?"

"Probably, but is that the kind of good time you want to show him? He'll refuse to go anywhere with you again."

"I guess you're right."

"Why are you hesitating?"

"We rented the boat for the entire night."

"You've got to be kidding." Shane tried to be sympathetic. He'd been in Hoyt's shoes himself not very long ago, completely inexperienced with kids and having to be taught. Luckily, Judy had been, and still was, patient with him. "Look, Benjie hardly knows you."

"I'm his father."

"Doesn't change the fact, until this weekend, you were a complete stranger."

"Yeah, well whose fault is that?"

Shane ignored the dig at Cassidy. "Look, she told me Benjie's never spent the night away from home except at her friend's house. This is all brand-new for him."

He heard Cheryl in the background seconding his suggestion. At least his sister-in-law was showing some sense.

"I don't want to take him home yet," Hoyt said firmly. "If I do, Cassidy will win."

"This isn't a contest."

"She'll deny me visitation."

What was with these people? Shane was ready to pull his hair out.

"Quit being selfish and bring your son home. Accept it's too soon for an overnight trip. Plan your next visit. Make peace with Cassidy."

He waited while Hoyt spoke to Cheryl, straining to decipher their murmured conversation. He made out nothing other than a word here and there.

"Okay," Hoyt finally said. "We're on our way."

"Good. I'll see you in the morning." Shane figured his brother and Cheryl would come around sometime before their flight left.

"Actually, we're going to head straight to the airport. It's been a tiring trip."

"What about Cassidy? Aren't you going to talk to her?"

"The less said the better."

"You're making a mistake."

"I'll see you in Payson next month."

"Benjie, come back here." Cheryl's voice rang out. "We're going home, but first we have to pack."

Where was the boy going? Weren't they still anchored at the marina? Shane jumped out of bed, wanting to do something and feeling helpless.

"Wait," Hoyt said. "Benjie wants to talk to you."

The next instant, his nephew's trembling voice said, "Uncle Shane?"

"Yeah, pal. How you doing?"

"I want to come home."

"You are. Your dad's promised. As soon as you're packed."

"He wouldn't let me call Mommy."

Poor decision on Hoyt's part. Had Benjie talked to Cassidy, he might not have had a meltdown, or as big a one. Hopefully, Hoyt had learned his lesson.

Benjie audibly swallowed a sob. "He doesn't like me."

"That's not true, pal. He loves you."

"He doesn't."

Shane's shoulders sagged. He'd badly wanted this initial meeting between Hoyt and Benjie to go as well as it had with his own daughter. And the frustrating part was it could have been great. Hoyt, as usual, allowed his excitement to overrule his good judgment.

"I want you to do me a favor," Shane told Benjie. "It's important."

"What?"

"I want you to give your dad another chance. Just because you didn't have fun this time, doesn't mean you won't the next. He's learning to be a dad, and you're learning to be his son."

"I guess."

"Good boy. Now, go on, help Cheryl pack so you can come home."

"Will you be there?"

The hope in Benjie's voice tore at Shane, and he regretted his answer. "Not tonight. But you can bet I'll see you tomorrow."

Cassidy, he was sure, wouldn't appreciate him being there. Plus, he didn't want to interfere in Hoyt's relationship with Benjie. Now that he thought about it, he and his nephew really should have a talk soon about how they could be the best of friends, but Hoyt was still Benjie's dad.

His brother took back the phone when Shane and Benjie were done. "Thanks for your help."

Unlike earlier, Hoyt sounded truly appreciative. Good. Maybe he was slowly coming around.

"Anytime."

After knocking around the trailer for the next ten minutes, Shane fell into bed, utterly spent—only to toss and turn. Wound up tighter than a spring, he grabbed a magazine and read until barking dogs, the low hum of an engine and distant voices alerted him that Hoyt and Cheryl had returned with Benjie.

Rising, he threw on some clothes and a warm jacket and ventured outside. His plan wasn't to barge in on the family, merely observe them from a distance.

From the corner of the barn, he watched Hoyt and Cassidy talking, their forms clearly illuminated in the beam of his brother's rental vehicle's headlights. Shane couldn't make out what they were saying, which he supposed was for the best. So far, they weren't yelling at each other. Benjie must have already gone inside. The poor kid was probably a wreck. Hell, they were all wrecks.

The minutes passed. If Shane had the sense of a gnat, he'd haul himself back to bed. He was further motivated when Cassidy turned to go inside the house. The discussion, whichever way it had gone, was over, and no one seemed any worse for it.

Shane started down the long barn aisle. He'd just reached the other end when a dark but distinctive figure emerged from the shadows.

"Mercer." Shane froze. "What are you doing out here in the middle of the night?"

"Same as you." Mercer stepped closer. There was no warmth in either his voice or manner. "Sunny called me."

"I'm glad Benjie's all right."

"That brother of yours, he doesn't know how lucky he is. If he ever tries anything like this again, I'll personally deck him."

Shane wasn't in the emotional frame of mind to debate his brother's behavior with Mercer. Not at two o'clock in the morning when they were both tired.

"He did the right thing in the end and brought Benjie home."

"He'd have been sorry if he hadn't."

"If you don't mind." Shane took a step. "I've got to be up in a few hours."

"One more thing." Mercer planted a hand in the center of Shane's chest.

"What?" He immediately went on the defensive and shook off the offending hand.

"I also heard about you and Cassidy. She's pretty distraught."

"Frankly, Mercer, it's none of your business."

"If it concerns my daughter, it is."

Before learning about Bria, Shane would have disagreed. Now, he understood and marginally lowered his guard.

"We had a misunderstanding."

"More like a knock down and drag out fight." Mercer's face hardened. "I warned you weeks ago you weren't to hurt her and, if you did, you wouldn't be working here anymore."

"Are you firing me?"

"I'm considering it."

Shane tensed. He needed this job. The chances were slim he'd find another one so well suited to him and close to Bria. But he wouldn't beg. He wasn't in the wrong.

"I hope you'll consider carefully. I'm a good bull manager."

"You've got one week to make it right."

With that, Mercer strode off in the direction of the house.

Make it right? Shane wasn't sure how to interpret his boss's remark. Did he want Shane and Cassidy to reconcile or did he want Shane to end things with her on good terms?

How could he decide when he wasn't sure himself what he wanted? Cassidy had changed, going from someone he thought he could possibly love to someone he barely knew.

TATUM'S TWO OLDEST children bailed out of Cassidy's vehicle the moment she came to a full stop in front of the elementary school.

"See you later," Drew called. He was a year behind Benjie, and the pair were practically inseparable. "You coming?" He waited for Benjie, who remained rooted in the middle back seat.

Cassidy studied her son's glum expression in the rearview mirror. "Give him a minute, will you, Drew?"

"Okay." The kindergartener hesitated, then, adjusting his backpack, joined his sister in the stream of students walking from the drop-off point to the school entrance.

"Want to tell me what's wrong?" Cassidy asked, though she had an inkling. Benjie had been out of sorts for most of the week, ever since the fishing trip fiasco.

"Uncle Shane says he and Bria aren't coming with us to Payson."

"He does, huh?"

Originally, Shane and his daughter were to accompany them on their visit to Hoyt at the Payson rodeo in March, turning the excursion into a family trip. But she and Shane had argued and barely spoken all week, ruining the plans.

He must have assumed he and Bria were no longer invited and told Benjie they was driving separately. Well, he'd assumed correctly. She wasn't ready to spend two days with him. She may never be ready.

"Why, Mommy?" Benjie asked.

She sighed, unsure how to answer.

Behind them, a horn beeped. Cassidy automatically checked her side mirror, noting the long line of vehicles waiting impatiently for their turn at the curb.

"I want him and Bria to go with us," Benjie whined.

"You can see her another time."

"You're being mean."

In his eyes, she probably was. Cassidy hadn't explained her argument with Shane to Benjie. She was, stupidly, hoping it wouldn't affect their relationship. Wrong, yes. She should practice what she preached and do what was best for her son. Except Shane had hurt her, and she wasn't ready to let bygones be bygones.

More than hurt her, he'd disappointed her and betrayed her, though the latter was a bit of a stretch. Still, she'd trusted him, which wasn't easy for her, and he'd let her down. He knew her fears. She'd told him during their most intimate moments, and he'd shown her he didn't care. Just because he felt a certain way, she was supposed to feel the same. Well, she didn't.

Five weeks ago, her life had been ordered and simple and routine. Now, she didn't know what was happening one minute to the next. And Shane was responsible. Like a tornado, he'd appeared and wreaked havoc, picking up the different pieces of her life, tossing them around and then dropping them. She had yet to stop reeling.

"I'm sorry, sweetie. I know it doesn't seem fair." She was about to say how parents sometimes had to make difficult decisions. Benjie's disappointed face had her reconsidering. "Maybe we can all drive up together. Let me see."

"Yay!" Benjie grabbed his backpack off the seat.

"No promises," she said, her words drowned out by the sound of the slamming rear door.

Benjie was gone in a flash.

Another sigh escaped. She would have continued to sit there, the engine idling, if a horn blast hadn't roused her.

"All right, already, I'm leaving." She threw the truck into gear.

Thanks to traffic letting up, the drive home was considerably quicker than the one to school, leaving Cassidy with less time to ponder her current dilemma than she'd have preferred.

How to approach Shane about the trip to Payson without him getting the wrong idea? Economics, she supposed. Why take two vehicles on the four-hour round trip when one would suffice? And with the children for company, she and Shane could avoid each other.

But wait. If they drove together, they'd have to stay at the same hotel overnight. Had he already made reservations? Damn, she should have thought this through more carefully before mentioning it to Benjie.

At the arena, she went straight to the office and found Tatum alone.

"How'd it go?" her friend asked. "The minions behave themselves?"

"They were fine." Cassidy sank into the visitor chair across from Tatum's desk, already exhausted and the day had hardly begun. "It's Shane. Well, not him. Benjie wanted to know why the four of us aren't driving together to Payson to see Hoyt."

Tatum laid down the monthly newsletter she'd been proofreading. "What did you tell him?"

"I'd talk to Shane about it."

"Good." She went back to reading.

"That's your only comment?"

"You two need to sort things out. You're both miserable, and this is a great icebreaker."

"I'm not miserable."

"Humph. Could've fooled me."

Cassidy sulked silently, fiddling with the buttons on her jacket.

After a moment, Tatum glanced up from the newsletter. "I'm not suggesting you make up. Actually, I am. But, at the least, you and Shane have to get along. Your children are cousins and friends."

"Is he really miserable?"

"And then some."

Cassidy sunk farther into the chair. "I don't care. It doesn't matter."

"You know, your father put him on probation."

"What?" She jerked upright.

"I overheard him telling your mom. Don't say anything to them."

"Forget it. I'm confronting Dad." Cassidy groaned. "The man knows no bounds, I swear."

"He's worried about you."

"Which is no reason for him to put Shane on probation. What happened between us has nothing to do with work." Mad as she was at Shane, she hadn't wanted this. Did he blame her? Probably. "I bet Mom gave Dad an earful."

"No. She agreed with him."

"I don't believe it." Cassidy pushed on the chair's arm rests, ready to hunt down her parents.

"Wait," Tatum said. "Before you go, I think you ought to ask yourself a question." She gave Cassidy a stern look. "Why are you so upset?"

"Why? Because I don't want him to lose his job, of course."

"And why don't you want him to lose his job?" Tatum persisted.

"Don't be ridiculous. He needs to work. He has a daughter to support. And living in Reckless puts him near Bria."

Tatum smiled with satisfaction. "How is it you can be so understanding of Shane and not Hoyt? He has a son and wants to be near him as much as possible."

"It's different with him."

"Not so different."

A tiny crack formed in Cassidy's defenses. Tatum had voiced aloud what Cassidy had been refusing to admit for days.

She sighed. "Okay, I get it. Hoyt just wanted to spend more time with Benjie. But he shouldn't have taken him without talking to me first."

"No one's arguing that." Tatum again put down the newsletter. "Speaking of which, how are the visitation negotiations going?"

"Hoyt had his attorney submit a schedule. I'm reviewing it now."

"And…"

"It's not unreasonable."

"You don't say."

"We are asking for a few adjustments."

Tatum's smile broadened. "Will wonders never cease? Two adults communicating and coming to a sensible, mutual agreement."

"Somehow I get the feeling you're not talking about me and Hoyt."

"Oh, I am. I just wish I was talking about you and Shane."

"I confess. Hoyt and I both acted badly. We allowed our emotions to get the better of us."

"You think?"

"But, Shane…" Cassidy couldn't go on. The pain had yet to lessen.

"The man is plumb crazy for you."

"Then why did he side with Hoyt against me?"

"Good grief!" Tatum clamped a hand to her forehead in frustration. "You think because he didn't completely, one-hundred-percent agree with you, he disagreed."

"Excuse me, but isn't that the definition of disagreeing?"

"Not at all. Nothing is ever black and white. Shane saw both sides, yours and Hoyt's, and understood them. He tried to be the mediator, encouraged you both to compromise, which, according to you, was a huge mistake."

"I was a little hard on him," Cassidy conceded.

"A little?"

"I was scared, all right?"

"I know, honey." Tatum's tone softened. "The last few weeks have been rough on you and a big adjustment. But the world hasn't ended. The thing you feared the most came and went, and you're still standing. Granted, with a few expected cuts and bruises. But you survived intact, other than losing a great guy you're head over heels in love with."

"Who said I was in love?" Cassidy asked in a small voice.

"You didn't have to. Anyone with half an eye can see it."

"It's too late for us," she said.

Tatum waved her off. "It's only too late if you let him leave."

"Leave?" Cassidy panicked. "Has he taken a new job?"

"If your dad fires him, he will."

Cassidy had made enough mistakes. She refused to be responsible for Shane losing his job. "Where are they?"

"If you're talking about your parents, they're at the livestock pens behind the arena. The team penning jackpot is tonight."

Cassidy didn't hear whatever else Tatum had to say. In the blink of an eye, she was out the office door and charging across the open area to the arena. Her parents must have sensed her coming for they turned in her direction well before she reached them. One look at their faces, at her father's arm around her mother's waist, and Cassidy instantly knew something was up.

"I'm glad you're here," her mother said after casting Cassidy's father a shy glance. "We have news."

Cassidy ground to a stop in front of them. "You finally said yes. You're getting married." It was, she supposed, inevitable.

"What!" Her mother blinked in surprise. "No, no."

"She's keeps stalling me," her father grumbled, then gave her mother a resounding peck on the cheek. "I'm moving into the house. This weekend."

"We thought you should be the first to know," her mother said.

Cassidy waited, expecting to be flooded with doubts and, possibly, anger. It didn't happen. Quite the opposite, in fact. She was overcome with—was this even possible?—contentment. "I'm glad for you."

"Are you sure?"

"Yes. In fact, I think it's great. As much as you fight, you're happier together than you are apart."

"That's how it usually is when you're in love."

Cassidy heard her father as if from a distance. The past weeks replayed in her mind. Shane's arrival at the Easy

Money. Their building attraction and fervent kisses. The night he took her to dinner at the Hole in the Wall.

He'd pushed her, it was true. Made her face her fears and do right by her son. He'd also been her friend, her lover and her confidant.

Tatum was right. This had been the hardest time of her life. It had also been the happiest she could remember. Because of Shane.

Cassidy did love him. Tatum was right about that, too. She loved him with all her heart.

Yet, she'd driven him away. Made them both miserable. Possibly cost him his job.

"I'm so pleased you're okay with it." Her mother beamed. "We were worried."

"Yeah, fine, whatever." She turned toward her father. "About Shane. You are not firing him, do you hear me?"

"Hell's bells, I'm not firing him. Where would I find a better bull manager?"

"I heard he was on probation."

Her father grimaced guiltily. "He might have been."

"But no longer?"

"I suppose I should tell him. The man's suffered long enough."

"You haven't!" Cassidy was appalled.

"When did you change your mind?" her mother asked, evidently not in the loop.

"A few days ago. After Benjie told me about the phone call."

"What call?" Cassidy and her mother asked simultaneously.

"According to Benjie, it was Shane who convinced Hoyt to bring him home last weekend. Hoyt wasn't going to at first."

"Shane did?" Cassidy's jaw dropped. "He never said a word."

"Did you give him the chance?"

No, she hadn't. "That doesn't explain why he wouldn't take the credit."

"You aren't the easiest person to approach."

From the time she was ten, she'd diligently kept people at a distance. What had it gotten her? She might have safeguarded her heart, but it had turned stone cold. She didn't want to live her life alone.

Tears blurred her vision. "I've spent years being afraid of nothing."

Her mother put an arm around her. "That seems to be the curse of this family."

"I've been awfully unfair to him."

"Tell him."

"He doesn't want anything to do with me." She struggled to bring her crying jag under control.

"I doubt it. He's still here."

Rather than drain her, Cassidy's outburst envigorated her. Was it possible for her perspective to change so quickly? Or had it been changing all along, day by day with Shane?

"Is he here?" She glanced around expectantly.

"Took the day off," her father said. "Mentioned some errands and picking up Bria."

His daughter. Shane was such a good father. The best. He would have been a good stepdad to Benjie, too. She and Shane had talked about it the mornings they'd woken up together. They could have had that every morning if she didn't mess up.

"He'll be back later this afternoon for the team penning jackpot."

Could Cassidy wait until then? Then again, what choice did she have?

Just her luck. She finally came to her senses, and Shane

wasn't around for her to first apologize and then ask him to forgive her fit of temper.

What if he refused? She had all day ahead of her to worry about it.

Chapter Fifteen

Shane automatically looked for Cassidy as he and Bria drove onto the arena grounds. It was a habit he'd gotten into well before they'd spent last weekend together. Probably from his first day at the Easy Money when he found her tidying his trailer.

"Can I go riding, Daddy?" Bria asked from the rear passenger seat, the doll she always brought with her lying across her lap.

"Sure. After we put your suitcase away."

Benjie wouldn't mind if she borrowed Skittles. The two children were close as, well, cousins. He'd be home from school soon. Maybe he'd join them. Shane decided to saddle up Rusty the mule just in case.

He'd have to check with Cassidy first, of course, fully aware he was manufacturing an excuse for them to talk. He'd been doing that a lot lately without much success. When she got mad at someone, she evidently stayed mad a good long time.

Damned if she wasn't infuriating. *And* addictive. When he wasn't wanting to rail at her, he wanted to kiss her till she begged him to stop. Never had he felt this strongly for a woman. She would be impossible to get over. Harder still when every night she visited his dreams and every day she invaded his thoughts.

He and Bria pulled up to the trailer and parked. He studied his temporary home while Bria scrambled from her car seat and ran inside. He'd need a new place soon. Real soon. A trailer was no place to raise a little girl. For a while, he'd thought maybe he, Cassidy and Benjie could find a house in Reckless. One with an extra room for Bria. That idea had gone up in smoke, and he had no one to fault but himself.

He'd told Cassidy he understood her fears and concerns and sympathized with them. The truth was, he hadn't. Not until it was too late. She and Hoyt weren't him and Judy. They were two different people with different histories and an entirely different relationship. He'd been wrong to assume Cassidy would feel and act like Judy or Hoyt like him, simply because their circumstances were similar. In hindsight, he should have done exactly what Cassidy needed and asked for: supported her unconditionally and gone to the marina, insisting Hoyt return Benjie home.

The mistake had cost him dearly.

Grabbing Bria's small suitcase and backpack from the floor of the truck, he carried both inside. At least he'd kept his job. Mercer had called earlier today to let Shane know he wasn't on probation anymore. Thank God for that much. Mercer hadn't offered an explanation, other than to say he'd spoken to Cassidy and all was well.

What did he mean? Shane would probably never find out.

Suitcase and backpack stowed in their usual place, Shane and Bria headed outside. She skipped along beside him to the stalls where Skittles and Rusty greeted them with lusty snorts and eager pawing.

"Up you go." Shane hoisted Bria onto Skittles's bare back.

She clutched the old horse's mane in her small hands

as he led the mounts to the main barn for brushing, saddling and bridling.

He was just finishing when Benjie came bounding down the aisle. Did the kid ever walk?

"No running, son," Shane called, not that he expected either Skittles or Rusty to react with anything more than a docile swishing of their tails.

"Can I go with you?" Benjie asked, grabbing Shane around the waist for a hug.

That was one quality Shane found appealing about his nephew. He always greeted Shane as if they hadn't seen each other for months instead of hours.

Two days ago, Shane had found a chance to speak with Benjie about their relationship, clarifying his role as uncle. Benjie had seemed to understand, which relieved Shane. He didn't want to confuse the boy further.

"I was planning on you coming along," he told Benjie, "but you'll have to ask your mom first."

"It's okay with me."

Shane swung around at the sound of Cassidy's voice. She was here! Within a few feet of him. Every cell in his body jumped to high alert. God, he'd missed her.

"Hey," he croaked, his throat having gone bone-dry.

She looked incredible, and not just because she was perpetually on his mind. There was something different about her. A glint in her eyes. A lightness to her step. A softness to her mouth that was in stark contrast to the thin, hard line of late.

What, he was desperate to know, accounted for the change? He had to find out.

"Can I talk to you?"

She smiled. Smiled! "I was about to ask you the same thing."

Shane didn't wait. He lifted Bria onto Skittles and settled her into the youth-size saddle. Benjie was already climbing onto Rusty.

"Come on," Benjie said to Bria once he was seated, and nudged the mule into a trot. "Race you."

Bria followed in hot pursuit before Shane could warn the boy to go slow.

"She takes after you," Cassidy said, watching the two children.

"They shouldn't run the horses down the barn aisle."

"Actually, they're trotting, not running. And I find it difficult to believe you never did anything like that at their age. I did."

"I plead the fifth."

This comfortable, casual banter was the kind of inter-action Shane had been hoping for with Cassidy. The kind they'd once shared. He'd rather there be more, but he'd accept friendship.

"What happened?" he asked when they reached the end of the aisle and stepped into the open area. "You're not mad anymore."

"I'm not sure where to begin."

"Try."

"An epiphany, I guess." She laughed quietly. "Or a severe reprimand from Tatum and my parents. They told me what I already knew."

"Sometimes we need to hear it from someone else."

She gazed up at him with those incredible, luminous dark eyes. "You're right."

All around them, the arena buzzed with activity. Students arriving for the afternoon riding classes. Vehicles and trailers hauling horses and participants for the team penning event. The Becketts, Mercer, Sunny, Ryder and Liberty, all hard at work. Benjie and Bria rode in the round pen, joined now by Tatum and her children who begged to ride double.

Home. Shane couldn't get the word out of his head. He'd felt as if the Easy Money was the right place for him and Bria from the day he'd arrived. Sooner, in fact. From the moment he'd driven across the town line into Reckless. Cassidy had been a large part of that.

"Is there any chance we can start over?" he asked.

"We should probably talk first."

Hope blazed inside him. She hadn't said no.

Before he could respond, she cradled his cheeks in her hands and drew him down for a full-blown, mouths-fused-together kiss. And, like each time before, she rocked his world.

A blank stare was all he could muster when she released him.

"You okay?" she asked.

"Uh, yeah." Was he? "What was that for?"

"Added insurance. In case you don't accept my apology."

"You have nothing to apologize for."

"I do. You've always been there for me. I was wrong to accuse you differently."

"I forced you to tell Hoyt about Benjie."

"I needed forcing. My family's a mess. *Was* a mess. I didn't want the same for Benjie and convinced myself that hiding him from Hoyt was the solution. It wasn't. Isn't."

The future Shane had thought lost to him appeared again on the horizon. "Things will work out with Hoyt."

"They will. Sooner or later. I'm committed. Hoyt is, too. We spoke last Thursday. Cleared the air. Set some ground rules we can both live with."

"I'm glad."

"Thank you." The glint was back in her eyes. "You've been a good friend and a good uncle to Benjie."

"I'd like to be more."

"I know. I wouldn't be here if I didn't."

He had to be sure he understood correctly, that she wanted what he did.

"Are you saying what I think you are?"

Her cheeks blushed a pretty pink Shane found sexy as all get-out. "I'd like for us to date."

He grinned. This was what he'd been waiting for. Praying for. "No."

"No?" She stumbled backward. "My mistake."

He captured her hand in his. "The only thing you're mistaken about is dating. I won't settle for that."

"I'm confused." She looked it, too.

He hauled her around the corner where they were out of sight.

"What about the kids?" she protested.

"Tatum's with them. They'll be all right for a minute, which is all the time I need."

"For what?"

"Cassidy." He dipped his head and nuzzled her ear. "I love you."

"It's too soon." She closed her eyes and trembled when he planted tiny kisses along the side of her neck.

"Are you saying you don't love me, too?"

"I…oh!"

"Yes?" He moved toward her mouth, ready to kiss a confession out of her. He didn't have to.

"I do," she whispered against his lips. "Love you—"

He cut her off with a searing hot kiss that went on and on. This was the missing piece, he thought through the haze surrounding his brain. The last one he needed to make his home, his life complete.

"Marry me," he said when they finally broke apart.

"You're crazy, you know." She laughed, the sound lovely and bright.

Shane lifted her by the waist and hauled her against him. "Is that a yes?"

"We can't."

"No?"

She became more serious. "What about your brother? How will he feel?"

Shane set her down, but he didn't let her go. "We'll figure it out."

"And Benjie and Bria. They're already confused. They'd go from being cousins to stepbrother and stepsister."

"Sweetheart, we can do this. Look at what your parents overcame. If they can work through their differences, we can, too."

She relaxed in his arms and he took heart. "I love you, and I'm committed to you and the family we'll have."

"We need to go slow," Cassidy insisted.

"Sounds reasonable. A month or two should do it."

"You're joking, naturally."

"A little." Shane kissed her again, this time a quick brush of his lips. He'd save the real celebration until later when they were alone. "I haven't met a woman yet I wanted to put a ring on her finger. Until you."

"Shane."

He could grow used to her saying his name like that. "Marry me, Cassidy. Soon. This summer. Next year. I don't care. As long as you do."

"Ah…" She kept him waiting another grueling few seconds before ending his agony. "Yes. But I do want to date awhile first."

Shane pulled her to him. "I'm going to make you happy. I swear it."

"You already have. You've given me the family I've always wanted and never thought was possible."

She'd taken the words right out of his mouth.

Epilogue

Three months later...

Cassidy flitted from one spot to the next, mentally checking off items. Cold hors d'oeuvres were laid out on trays, hot ones warmed in chafing dishes. The caterers were busy in the kitchen, putting the finishing touches on the barbecue dinner. A four-tier cake sat on a table by the window, the top adorned with a miniature cowboy groom and cowgirl bride. A three-piece band was setting up in the backyard and tuning their instruments.

The wedding, the biggest one ever hosted at the Easy Money, had gone off without a hitch. The newly married couple was outside, finishing up with the reception line. They'd be here soon, and the reception would begin.

"There you are."

Cassidy felt Shane's arms come from behind to circle her waist.

"Hi." She leaned into him, weak in the knees from loving him so much and being loved in return.

He'd been her biggest helper in putting on this wedding. Cassidy didn't know if she had the strength for the next one. The Becketts were getting hitched right and left. That was one of the reasons she'd decided to take her time becoming Mrs. Shane Westcott. Plus, they were still developing their unique blended family.

Benjie and Hoyt had made considerable progress since the fishing trip. Their visit in Payson two months ago had gone well and there was a second one in the works for May.

Bria accepted Cassidy as her father's girlfriend, and the two were becoming close. For now, she called Cassidy "Auntie," which made sense to her because Benjie was her cousin. Cassidy was fine with that and didn't care if it ever changed.

Make no mistake, however, she would marry Shane. Their time together had shown her what life could be like, spent side by side with the man of her dreams.

They'd finally found a house this week. The purchase would be finalized next month, and then they'd move in. She, Benjie, Shane and, on every other weekend, Bria. They were a family, happy and close-knit.

"Here they come," someone shouted, and the crowd separated to make a path for the bride and groom. "Mr. and Mrs. Beckett."

Cassidy's parents, all smiles and radiating joy, entered through the door, their arms linked and the photographer snapping pictures.

"Mr. and Mrs. Beckett again!" someone else said.

Her parents laughed unabashedly.

Cassidy laughed, too. More than accepting her parents' spur-of-the-moment nuptials, she was delighted. They'd come full circle, all of them. What had started nearly a year ago as Liberty seeking her biological father had ended with the Becketts becoming complete. Whole. Healed. A family in the truest sense of the word.

It was the greatest gift Cassidy could have hoped to receive.

"Liberty and Deacon are next," Shane said.

"Three months from now."

Ryder and Tatum had exchanged their vows last month in a small, quiet service. Today, with her pregnancy clearly showing, she'd sat beside Ryder, along with the rest of the family, during the ceremony.

"Can I talk you into finally setting a date?" Shane turned Cassidy inside the circle of his arms, then gave her a light kiss. "The kids are getting anxious."

"The kids couldn't care less."

Benjie and Bria were at that moment playing with Tatum's brood under the watchful eye of the sitter Cassidy had hired.

"Don't make me wait too long."

"Or what?" Cassidy smiled up at Shane. What had she done to deserve this man?

"Ever hear of a shotgun wedding?"

"I think you have it backward. A shotgun wedding is when the groom is forced to marry the bride."

"A technicality."

She'd been determined to wait, at least until this summer, to decide. Suddenly, she wanted nothing more than to have her future set. It must be the mood of the day.

"I've always thought a June wedding would be nice."

Shane's head snapped up. "Next month? Really!" He broke into a grin. "All right."

"No, no. A year from next month."

"Too long," he insisted.

"I'll make the wait worth it."

"I'm holding you to that." He reached into his pocket. "Guess I can give this to you now. Been carrying it around for weeks."

He took her left hand and slipped the diamond and ruby ring onto her finger.

She blinked back tears. "It's beautiful." More beautiful than she could have imagined. "I love it."

"And I love you."

While everyone surrounded the newlyweds, Shane swept Cassidy away to a secluded corner of the house, where they sealed their brand-new engagement with kisses promising a lifetime of happiness.

* * * * *

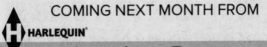
#1557 TEXAS REBELS: FALCON

Texas Rebels • by Linda Warren

Falcon Rebel's wife, Leah, did the unthinkable: she left him and their three-month-old baby. Now she's back, wanting to see her daughter. Will Falcon allow her into their lives again or refuse to give her a second chance?

#1558 FALLING FOR THE SHERIFF

Cupid's Bow, Texas • by Tanya Michaels

Kate Sullivan is busy raising her teenage son, and she has no interest in dating again. But single dad Cole Trent, the sheriff of Cupid's Bow, Texas, may make her change her mind!

#1559 THE TEXAS RANGER'S WIFE

Lone Star Lawmen • by Rebecca Winters

To protect herself from a dangerous stalker, champion barrel racer Kellie Parrish pretends to be married to Cy Vance, the hunky Texas Ranger assigned to her case. But it's impossible to keep their feelings about each other completely professional...

#1560 THE CONVENIENT COWBOY

by Heidi Hormel

Cowgirl Olympia James only agreed to marry her onetime fling Spence MacCormack to help him keep custody of his son. But when she discovers she's pregnant—with Spence's baby—this convenient marriage might turn into something more.

REQUEST YOUR FREE BOOKS!
2 FREE NOVELS PLUS 2 FREE GIFTS!

Ⓗ HARLEQUIN®

American Romance®

LOVE, HOME & HAPPINESS

SPECIAL EXCERPT FROM

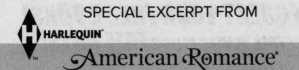

HARLEQUIN

American Romance®

*Falcon Rebel hasn't seen Leah in seventeen years…
but he's never forgotten her.*

*Read on for a sneak preview of
TEXAS REBELS: FALCON,
the second book in Linda Warren's
exciting new series TEXAS REBELS.*

A truck pulled up to the curb and her thoughts came to an abrupt stop. It was Falcon.

There was no mistaking him—tall, with broad shoulders and an intimidating glare. She swallowed hard as his long strides brought him closer. In jeans, boots and a Stetson he reminded her of the first time she'd met him in high school. Being new to the school system, she was shy and didn't know a lot of the kids. It took her two years before she'd actually made friends and felt like part of a group. Falcon Rebel was way out of her group. The girls swooned over him and the boys wanted to be like him: tough and confident.

One day she was sitting on a bench waiting for her aunt to pick her up. Falcon strolled from the gym just as he was now, with broad sure strides. She never knew what made her get up from the bench, but as she did she'd dropped her books and purse and items went everywhere. He'd stopped to help her and her hands shook from the intensity of his dark eyes. From that moment on there was no one for her but Falcon.

Now he stood about twelve feet from her, and once again she felt like that shy young girl trying to make conversation. But this was so much more intense.

Be calm. Be calm. Be calm.

"I'm…I'm glad you came," she said, trying to maintain her composure because she knew the next few minutes were going to be the roughest of her life.

His eyes narrowed. "What do you want?" His words were like hard rocks hitting her skin, each one intended to import a message. His eyes were dark and angry, and she wondered if she'd made the right decision in coming here.

She gathered every ounce of courage she managed to build over the years and replied, "I want to see my daughter."

He took a step closer to her. "Does the phrase 'Over my dead body' mean anything to you?"

Don't miss TEXAS REBELS: FALCON by Linda Warren, available August 2015 wherever Harlequin® American Romance® books and ebooks are sold.

www.Harlequin.com

HAREXP0715

THE WORLD IS BETTER
WITH
Romance

Harlequin has everything from contemporary, passionate and heartwarming to suspenseful and inspirational stories.

**Whatever your mood,
we have a romance just for you!**

Connect with us to find your next great read, special offers and more.

f /HarlequinBooks

🐦 @HarlequinBooks

www.HarlequinBlog.com

www.Harlequin.com/Newsletters

HARLEQUIN®

A *Romance* FOR EVERY MOOD™

www.Harlequin.com